INTO THE PINES

RYAN LILL-WASHINGTON

Blurbs

"Ryan Lill-Washington is a major talent to watch. Fierce, rhapsodic, imaginative, and enthralling as a thunderstorm, this dazzling Queer storyteller is forging a sensation path in genre fiction"

-**Margot Douaihy**, Author of SCORCHED GRACE

"Ryan Lill-Washington is a truly magical storyteller. He wields his words like a sword, slicing away at any expectations to reveal a veritable mountain of talent and wisdom. Readers will find themselves unable to put Into The Pines down for even a moment. (Sleep? I don't know her.) He proves himself to be a brilliant writer with every page and personally, I am eager to devour anything he serves up."

-**Alaina Urquhart**, Author of the New York Times Best-selling Novel THE BUTCHER AND THE WREN, co-host of MORBID PODCAST

Mom,

This book is dedicated to you. You cry when you see trees being cut down. You may be ridiculous, but you're also the best. Thank you for introducing scary books, horror films, and true crime to me. But most of all, thank you for showing up in the front row of my bullshit. Thank you for giving me the space to grow into who I am, and for never doubting that I could succeed, even when I didn't believe I could.

PREFACE

I love the woods. I always have. There has always been a part of me that thinks everything in the wilderness is magical. Magical, but terrifying. The ecosystem, the hierarchy of predators, and the beauty of a landscape. I have always loved the woods, but I've also always been afraid of them. The thought that you never truly know if you're alone. Every time I have found myself enjoying the wonders that lie within the woods, I also find myself second-guessing my decisions and wondering if I'm being watched. The moment I turn around, I immediately find myself thinking that someone could be right behind me, ducking behind the trees as I search for them.

I love the woods. I always have.

Chapter One

Girl in The Pines

The ground was soft under her feet now, wet from the early morning dew. She couldn't feel the cuts along her feet anymore, not since going off the trail's edge. The muscle-tearing cramps from her thighs had started to subside, but she couldn't stop running, not yet.

The trees curved inward towards each other, barricading the small amounts of sun trying to push through the trees. The further she ran, the thicker the forest became, closing in around her from every side. The small tree limbs from the brush made contact with her skin, pulling and scratching her, opening small cuts, and tangling her hair. She pushed forward, slapping at the tangles of thorns and dead limbs pulling her back. The cuts covering her body worked their way up her arms, barely covered by the torn jean shirt she still wore, the sleeves shredded and outlined in her blood. Most of her wounds from the night before were dry now, but every branch she made contact with pulled a little more at her skin, reopening the cuts.

It didn't matter how tired she was, this wasn't the moment to give up, not now. If she could survive what happened the night before then she could survive this.

A road, that's all she could think about now. A road, a path, a trail, something. Any sign or sight of one would be enough to keep her hopeful.

The woods were loud, the sounds of branches cracking and screaming birds surrounded her in neverending noise. There was no peace here, only fear. The ground was starting to feel softer, parts giving way when her foot made contact with it, pulling her into the Earth as she ran. The harder she pushed forward, the deeper her feet sank into the ground, slowing her run to a crawl.

Swamp, it was everywhere here, and came out of nowhere when you least expected. The woods in South Carolina weren't just filled with beautiful trees and autumnal colors, they were laced with hidden spots of wet Earth, crawling with creatures lurking beneath the leaves that didn't care why you were there. The tall pines that grew here were surrounded by smaller trees and brush, thorn bushes, and weaving vines. Any direction you ran in had its own set of punishments awaiting you, it didn't matter how fast you went.

She lifted her legs out of the sinking ground, falling forward onto her hands. Her head snapped up, looking left to right, behind her, above her, and before her. A white cloud of fog moving along the forest floor in front of her snapped her back to reality for just a moment. Run, it's the only thing you can do. *The fog could hide me*, she thought, *the fog could cover me. Get to the fog!* She pushed off of the ground and started to run, the muscles in her legs starting to contract. The cramps would return if she stayed still for too long, and if she stopped, that was it. It didn't matter how badly it hurt, it didn't matter how far it was, if she didn't run, she would be dead next. She hated the woods. If she ever made it out she swore she would never step foot into them again.

This had all been a mistake, a huge mistake. She should never have come to this place. No one would care about another girl missing in the Pines.

CHAPTER TWO

EYVETTE

It was Thursday night when Charlie's mom finally called me back. I was glued to my phone, anxiety filling my veins every time I felt it vibrate. I had been waiting for her phone call for days.

The motel I stopped at was a dingy-looking place, the type of shitshow you find on the less traveled roads off the side of the interstate, scattered across the outskirts of towns that no one cared to visit anymore. The walls were paneled with wood, spotty and damaged from the cracking of the original lacquer that was being eaten off by time. I had yet to unpack my suitcase, uncertain of how long I would be staying here, always ready to leave at a moment's notice.

I positioned myself on the edge of the bed, my feet barely able to touch the yellow and brown stained carpeting that covered the room from wall to wall. This was my one chance to gather as much information as I could, and I couldn't risk missing her call, anxiety or not.

When I answered, I tried to sound as somber as I could. Her voice was weak and heavy, the sounds of a mother who hadn't been able to get any sleep in weeks.

Three days ago, I had driven back to this place in search of answers, in search of Charlene Ellis, the second of the girls to go missing in the Pines this year. Charlene, or "Charlie" to me and those who knew her, had gone missing while on a solo backpacking weekend almost three weeks ago. I had to be careful how I handled this conversation and I knew that. On one hand, I had a complicated and drama-filled history with Charlie. I knew her mother and father from years of sleepovers and girl's nights and had also gone to school with her annoying younger brother, Jeff.

On the other hand, I wasn't just Eyvette Thompson from small-town South Carolina anymore. No, I was Yvee Thompson now. Girlfriend to up-and-coming actress Izzy Chambers and host of "The Last Cassette Tape" podcast, which had more than exploded in the last year. With our less-than-friendly history, I knew that it wouldn't be easy speaking to her.

I tried to exchange pleasantries, hoping that I could feel out whether or not she was open to a personal conversation with me after all of this time. I hadn't spoken to Dorene Ellis in years and, up until three weeks ago, I would have never thought to speak to her again.

Our last encounter was less than pleasant, ending in a shouting match outside of her front door, Charlie screaming at her to "stay out" of our business. A kiss between the two of us had been seen by her father, after months of dating secretly, sending her mother into a tailspin during dinner.

I always wondered why he felt the need to bring it up that night, instead of just asking me about it later. I had always liked Joe, but the moment he saw the two of us, his face changed into something I couldn't figure out.

I couldn't pinpoint whether he was having trouble reconciling that his daughter was potentially a lesbian or battling the fact that I wasn't white.

Whatever his reasoning, it always felt personal to me.

It wasn't a moment of pride in my history, and I wish we were speaking under better circumstances, but here we were. Her silence on the phone told me that I was going to have to work extra hard to get any information out of her that I could find helpful. I almost felt bad, using my personal connection to her for help, but if it meant that I could solve any of this, it would be worth it.

The bed underneath me was squeaky, the springs almost visible through the sheets covering the mattress. I originally thought about pulling them off to examine the bed but decided it was probably best not to know what was hidden under the covers. I stood up, deciding that sitting on the bed wasn't giving me enough stability to make me comfortable enough to start asking Mrs. Ellis the questions I needed answered.

"I'm really sorry I couldn't make it back for the search, Mrs. Ellis," I said to her softly. "I have been so incredibly busy with–" she cut me off before I could even finish my apology.

"What is it that you want, Eyvette?" she asked, voice stern and short.

I was a bit taken aback and fumbled over my words before I could make another sentence. No one called my Eyvette anymore, they hadn't for a long time now.

"Well, Mrs. Ellis, I'm actually here now, back in South Carolina," I said to her.

"Well bless your heart," she started. "What brings you back to these parts?" she asked me, her voice starting to venture into the annoyance of me. I could tell she knew exactly why I was there.

"I'm here for Charlie," I told her. "I'm here to find her." It sounded almost like I had knocked the breath out of her, and it took her a moment to clear her throat before she responded to me.

"Charlene has been missing for over three weeks, and you think you're going to come back here and find her now? Why? How? How would you know anything about where she could be, Eyvette?" She no longer sounded like a frail mother, agonizing over her daughter's disappearance, but an angry woman ready to lay into someone.

I understood it, but I wasn't to blame for Charlie having gone missing.

"I knew her," I said softly, "and I know how much she loved it out here. I'm going to try at least." I used to know her, that was true, and she did love it out here, it was her favorite place on Earth. She was constantly trying to drag us out here on weekends, exploring all the trails that led their way up toward North Carolina.

"You haven't spoken to her in years, hun. I only called you back to tell you to leave us be. Go home, Eyvette, everyone knows exactly what you're doing here. No one is going to tell you anything that could be used on your horrible little show," she snapped back at me. "How dare you come back here to use her."

I took a moment, gathering myself before I tried to reply, but all I got was a deep breath before she ended the call.

I sat back down on the bed, still holding my phone up to my ear, and released another deep breath through closed teeth. *Fuck, that hadn't gone well at all*, I thought, yet it went exactly how I expected it to.

She wasn't wrong. I did sometimes feel like I was just using Charlie's disappearance, but after the last three weeks at home and the long drive down here, I decided that I was doing this for the right reasons. She had been such a large part of my life, such a large part of the reason I left this town. If it hadn't been for her, I wouldn't have ever pushed myself into the career I wanted, and I would have never gone to Los Angeles or had the courage to come out of my comfort zone and live authentically. At least I had done that.

Charlie had spent the last few years of her life on the road as a traveling nurse, her Instagram constantly changing locations and displaying beautiful cityscapes. She would write in her captions how much she missed the wilderness, but that the city was just like the woods, filled with all types of creatures and beauty.

She and I unblocked each other only a few years back, probably both just wanting to check in and see if the other was the same after all that time had passed.

I hadn't even known she was missing until Izzy shoved her phone in my face one night, gasping aloud after having come across her flier detailing her last whereabouts on an Instagram thread currently trending. I quickly grabbed my phone and swiped through her profile, checking the last few photos and videos she posted, hoping that they would give me some kind of insight into her life or what happened to her.

They hadn't.

It was just more of the same, over and over again, buildings and quotes about traveling. My inbox was overflowing with listeners from the podcast, some kind, some hateful. I hadn't noticed her message to me from a month ago letting me know she was going home for a long weekend to hike and it made her think of me. I showed the message to Izzy, shaking my head in disbelief that she was missing.

Charlene Ellis wasn't the first girl to go missing in the woods here. There were always people getting lost in the forest, usually stumbling across another camper after a day or two spent wandering aimlessly in circles, normally finding help. But these disappearances were different.

Summer brought with it the first of the missing girls yet to be found: Meredith Bates, a school teacher from Tennessee who had traveled down to the Carolinas on a group camping trip with a few coworkers. The news reported that two of the coworkers had awoken in the middle of the night and found her tent unoccupied, backpack, water bottle, and flashlight all missing.

Within 24 hours, a search team spread out across the forest, covering miles upon miles of ground, but not a single trace of her was found. Theories began to sprout, from local ghost stories to murderers living in the woods, to alien abductions or faking her own death. The media went wild with coverage, her face and name plastered on every magazine, newspaper, and television program they could get to follow the story. The image of her with a backpack slung over one shoulder, long brown hair up in a messy bun with a red bandana with a school logo on it.

Her husband gave multiple interviews, swearing that their home life was a happy one and she had no reason to leave her job, friends, marriage, or life. He joined in on the search, which lasted a little over two weeks, until they called it off, unable to find the answers we all wanted. There was no physical evidence to suggest she had just walked away, and there were hundreds of miles of woods that she could have disappeared into if she wanted to.

As the weeks went by, her missing posters faded along the walls of buildings and street signs, and the media moved on to the next awful thing happening in the world. It wasn't until three weeks ago that the frenzy picked up again, naming Charlene Ellis as the second girl to go missing within the Pines.

I sat in silence for a moment, remembering a conversation I had with Charlie on the outskirts of town before.

The first time she brought me here, I was terrified. I had grown up only a few miles from here, but I wasn't a camper or a backpacker, and I had never spent any time in the woods. We were 15 years old and had somehow been granted permission to go camping for the weekend by our parents.

When we drove up to the woodsy area surrounding town, a sense of dread had washed its way over my body. She picked jokes at me, and told me not to worry, that the woods were beautiful, and that I was going to love this place so much I wouldn't want to go home. She laughed as we pulled into the gravel lot of the entrance to the trail and slapped my thigh.

I tried to remember exactly what she said to me while she was unloading the bags from the back of her Dad's car, but the words weren't coming to me. She tossed me a hiking bag, my water bottle, then slammed the trunk shut. We only had a few hours until the sun was going down, but she assured me that we would have our camp set up and be ready when the time came. I was comforted in knowing she wasn't afraid and followed her through the archway of trees, into the forest.

Now, she was out there somewhere and no one had been able to find her. I was going to look in all the places she took me, all the places she could have potentially left clues to her whereabouts. It was a long shot, but if she was still out there, someone needed to find her. Tomorrow morning, I would head out into the woods and look for any traces of her.

The thought sent a small wave of anxiety across my body as I laid back on the motel bed. I hadn't been here in so long and I'd never been into the woods alone. My thoughts shot back to Izzy telling me not to get lost out here.

I closed my eyes and drifted to sleep.

Chapter Three

Eyvette

The idea of a podcast seemed so unbelievably daunting to me when it was originally suggested. Me, solo, in front of a mic for hours a week, talking to strangers? No, no way in hell. I was perfectly content jumping between odd jobs amidst Izzy's auditions. But after moving to Los Angeles, our relationship had been blasted into the tabloids, causing almost nightly fights.

While Izzy's career was blossoming into everything she dreamed it could be, I was still struggling to find my footing in a new city. I spent week after week searching for work. I'd check local classifieds and job listings, yet none of them panned into anything serious. It was frustrating.

The constant search for work, relying on Izzy to cover all of the expenses, with absolutely no future prospects began to take its toll on me mentally. Izzy always said that she didn't mind, but having someone paying for my existence felt incredibly uncomfortable.

She would come home from set, bubbly and happy, immediately asking how my day was and if I found something more permanent. I knew that she didn't mean it to sound condescending, but every time she asked I felt more and more disappointed in myself. It wasn't until her publicist came over for dinner one weekend that the idea of the podcast was suggested.

"You know, Eyvette...I have a few connections in broadcasting and they're always looking for new voices," Penelope suggested. She too was always excited, her personality louder than Izzy's.

"What do you mean, like radio?" I asked her, laughing as I did.

"No, more like a bunch of podcasts. They do all kinds of genres. If you're interested, I have a few people there I could get in touch with," she told me.

"Oh, babe, that would be perfect for you!" Izzy chimed in from the kitchen. "You're always talking about music and about how you wanted to be an MTV host when you were a kid!" She laughed and I shot her a look of slight embarrassment.

"Yeah, when I was *kid*, Iz," I said, my eyes squinting at her with fake anger.

She laughed and walked back to the table with another bottle of wine.

"Listen, no pressure. I just know you've been looking and this is just an option," Penelope offered.

"I appreciate it, really," I told her, "I just don't know if anyone wants to talk about music that much."

"Bullshit," Izzy laughed, setting the wine bottle on the table and pulling up on the cork with all of her body weight.

I reached over and grabbed it from her.

"Give me that," I laughed. I pulled the cork out and handed her the bottle of red wine back.

"Oh, you think you're so strong, huh?" She joked at me, blowing me a kiss across the table. Penelope laughed and the night went on without another mention of me trying to find work.

Izzy landed a major role in a new hit television series the following week, which meant steady work for her through a studio for the foreseeable future. I was happy for her, but the positive news also hit a nerve.

I felt like so much was being handed to her and she always seemed so shocked when she received a callback that she was cast. I was never the type of person to feel jealous or petty about someone else's success, but everything just seemed to come so easy for her. I was more envious than jealous that she had the confidence to walk into a building, read lines off to a stranger, then wait around for them to let her know if she was good enough or not. I wished I dared to put myself out there as she could, but I had always been the quieter of the two of us.

When we first met I had no idea who she was. After she initially approached me to tell me she liked the way I styled my hair I blurted out some type of thanks and walked away. Two of my old coworkers, who had invited me out to what I believed was a pity lunch, demanded to know how I knew Izzy Chambers. I explained to them that not only did I not know who she was, I had no clue who they were talking about. They pointed back to the girl who had complimented me, still looking in my direction, giving a small wave and smiling my way. I waved back, sending my coworkers into a tailspin of delight.

She hovered around a few minutes near the coffee counter before she approached the table and dropped a small note with her number on it. She was the most beautiful girl I had ever seen, her dark skin almost perfect and shimmering, and, for some reason, she was attracted to me.

It only took a week of Izzy coming home from the set, with incredible stories about how wonderful her castmates and directors were, before I reached out to Penelope about the idea of the podcast. She agreed to meet me for lunch and suggested that I have ideas ready to submit. She would only open the lines of communication with her connections, but it was up to me to really "sell" myself to them.

The idea of having to promote my own ideas was daunting, but I knew I could only handle watching Izzy's success for so long before it would destroy the relationship we were building. Things intensified when the show started running its promotions, throwing Izzy's face across the television every time we tried to watch something. She was on the cover of magazines and previews and, somehow, I was thrown inside the interview, labeled as the lowly girlfriend of an up-and-rising star.

During lunch, Penelope listened to all of my ideas and we settled on a podcast focused on the last song people listened to before they died. A mixture of music and true crime splashed with a hint of comedic relief. It sounded easy enough, but I knew it was going to take weeks of prep work, gathering information, and plotting out storylines before each and every episode.

I didn't wait around for a response from her connections. Instead, I went out immediately after our lunch and purchased all the necessary equipment to run my own podcast on the one small credit card I owned. I stopped inside a local tech shop and the nice man behind the counter talked me into buying all sorts of things that would make me sound "legit." I got home and decided that our guest room was going to be my new podcasting room.

With a fresh coat of paint and a cheap "build it yourself" desk from online, I was ready to go.

That was all it took for me to dive into it, beginning my research with a few local murders that had taken place within the last year. I spent days tracking down friends and family members of the deceased on social media, connecting the dots to find the last person they spent time with. From that, I would narrow down each person's last movements and find out if they remember any music playing. I would do my best to find their last played song on social media or online playlists, something they may have listened to just before their death.

At first, I found myself feeling slightly uncomfortable asking people questions about music. Some were hopeful I was somehow going to crack a case that the police had yet to solve, but when the conversation shifted to music I could audibly hear their confusion and disappointment. Not everyone was upset or angry, in fact, some of the people really enjoyed telling tales about how much that person had loved music or movies. I would let them ramble on, jotting down as much information as I could to add meat to the podcast episode. I spent my days sifting through stories, sometimes letting myself drift so far into these people's lives that I would forget to eat.

Their stories meant something, and the simple fact that I could tie them into something I cared about made it even more fascinating for me. The more I pushed into it, the further down the rabbit hole of true crime I went. I settled on using a small podcast platform I paid a monthly subscription for and I decided to put out an episode, just to see what it could potentially do.

The morning I released it, I sent it out into the world of social media, unaware it would explode into what it is now. It wasn't until Izzy came in from a day of shooting that I even knew what was happening online.

I was brewing a pot of coffee in the afternoon, still sweaty from a bit of yoga I had done after recording more bits for the show. Some followers of hers saw my post and shared it, and it was blasted further into the social media world. Not only had it been shared by some of her fans, but multiple news sources picked it up and were running a story on it.

I sat in disbelief as Izzy scrolled through countless pages of remarks regarding the first episode of the podcast. I was having trouble coming up with a name the entire time I was recording clips, but had settled on "The Last Cassette Tape" and the title had stuck with the people online.

By the end of its first day out, I was receiving multiple offers from online podcasts and radio shows, some even offering to buy the title and idea. Penelope dropped by the house, hastily ready to offer her services to me.

"You're going to need someone to help you with all of this," she said excitedly.

"I am?" I asked her, still in shock from all the attention it was getting.

"Absolutely! You're going to want to promote as much as you can! This is huge! You're on the top of the charts right now and it's only been a *day*!" She jumped up and down in excitement, reaching out to me for a hug.

I stepped into it and joined in on the jumping sarcastically.

"So, what now?" I asked her, finally feeling good about something I was doing.

"The sky's the limit, baby!" Penelope proclaimed.

Izzy joined in the jumping, hopping up and down towards me until her hands met my shoulders.

"My girl's gonna be famous, she's gonna be famous," she started singing loudly while laughing.

I laughed along, the thought of fame seemed so uncomfortable to me.

We settled down at the table and Penelope launched into all the ways she could take this higher for me.

"Listen, right now you own all of your own rights, so you're making all of your own money. There's no need to join teams with anyone if you have my help promoting and watching your back!" She seemed so confident in what she was telling me.

I agreed to let Penelope help me with the launch of the second episode and I showed her what I had planned for the next few recording sessions.

"You really think this could be something?" I asked, my face showing just how insecure I was feeling.

"Hell yes!" she shouted across the table. "I know it will!"

Almost a year into the release of "The Last Cassette Tape" I was still top of the streaming charts and just finished the first part of my series with a three-part episode that covered my 15th crime of the year. Izzy and I were happy, both avoiding any scrutiny in the tabloids and enjoying our collective careers, which were both on the rise.

It wasn't until a month after my last episode aired, that rumors of my show being in the middle of a lawsuit were blasted to the front of the headlines.

It wasn't true, not completely at least.

A mother of one of the victims featured on my show refuted the evidence that I brought forward about her son's last song. To me, it hadn't been any different than the other episodes I released. I told the story of what happened to her son the night he was killed in a three-part arch and found out from friends who had left him at a party alone that his last song was "Teenage Dream" by Katy Perry. It wasn't until the online community started on its rampant rage of online sleuthing and homophobia that his mother realized her son, who had not come out publicly, was the target of a hate crime.

This case, along with one other, had been reopened due to my show and led to the arrest of a local man who finally admitted to killing her son to keep him quiet about their affair. He was a married man afraid of being outed. She wasn't suing me, but she had come forward about how "tacky" my show was for airing out her son's private information. People online were torn between congratulating me for helping solve his murder and blaming me for outing someone.

While that hadn't been my intention, I took the backlash with a grain of salt and released a statement that identity in oneself is of the utmost importance to me, and that I would never want to hurt our community, having felt like such an outcast my entire life. It had mostly calmed down, but his mother wasn't letting it go, constantly re-posting things about me, bringing more vitriol to my pages.

Penelope and Izzy told me it was probably best to just lay low for a while and let the news move on to something different. However, Penelope also thought that with all the press surrounding the podcast, it was best to keep pushing out content. She believed that there was no such thing as bad press, and often reminded me of it.

It had been her idea to investigate the disappearance of Charlie, the second of two girls to go missing in the Pines near my hometown. I originally told her there was no way in hell I was going back there. Nothing good ever came from me being in South Carolina, especially now. I no longer had ties there and anyone I used to know, no longer spoke to me.

After the podcast skyrocketed, I became another pariah in my hometown, exploiting people for money and fame, at least that's what the magazines said when some reporter came here to do a story on Izzy and myself.

Penelope told me that this would be my chance to "rebrand the podcast" and really get my hands dirty with the research. It was personal and people would love that. It was a type of marketable that people couldn't put a price tag on.

I rolled my eyes at her, but she kept pushing the idea, slamming a newspaper clipping of Charlie down in front of me, her green eyes bright in the missing photo. Izzy wasn't on board with the thought of me going back home, nor did she care for Penelope pushing me to investigate an old flame of my past. It didn't feel like that to me, but she would often compare it to something that had offended me at the beginning of our relationship just to make her point.

"You didn't like it when Sarah wanted to grab coffee with me," Izzy spat towards me, her hands on her hips.

"That's different, Iz, you'd just broken up not long ago," I said, giving her an "Are you serious" kind of look.

She doubled down, refusing to see the difference between the two situations.

"It's not different. You liked her and she liked you, it doesn't matter if you two were never publicly dating, it still counts!"

"Penelope thinks it's a good idea for the podcast," I told her, trying to shake the entire thing off.

Her eyes narrowed, eyebrows raised at me.

"Penelope is a white girl who only sees dollar signs!" she countered, causing us both to start laughing. It was true, she was very much that type of girl, too privileged to see the potential harm in all of it. "And that's just what we need, Yvee, you getting your Black ass lost in the woods!"

"I've been in those woods a hundred times!" I said, trying to stop myself from laughing again.

"Uh huh, now two white girls are missing and you think going back to bum fuck South Carolina is going to help them? How? Those people don't care about you," she said, her eyebrows still raised. She was serving up as much attitude as she could muster.

I walked towards her, wrapping my arms around her waist.

"I promise, it will be fine," I told her.

She let out a long exhale and melted into my arms.

"You always do this," she grumbled. "You always fight dirty." Her lips touched mine and the problem was settled, for the time being.

Chapter Four

Girl in The Pines

The forest slowly disappeared behind her the further she made her way into the fog, the warmth of it wrapping itself around her. Every breath she took felt like a mouthful of water entering her lungs. The muscles in her legs were starting to pull harder than before, stretched close to their limit. The pain made its way up the backs of her thighs, across her lower back, and radiated up to her neck.

She had run all night, the darkness covering her, from the moment she was able to get away. The trees in front of her opened up into a small ravine, a steady trickle of water making its way through the hollowed-out section of forest. Large roots were protruding from the ground, creating a small opening into the Earth, with a curtain of root ropes hanging before it.

She made her way towards it, falling into the pool of water before she could catch herself. Her wounds stung as the dirty water splashed over her, the stains on her denim shirt bleeding red out into the stream.

Reaching out towards the root ropes, she pulled herself into the small opening, turning her back into the ground and pulling her legs in towards her chest. The cramps took over her legs and she clasped her hands over her mouth to stop from screaming, kicking out each leg in an attempt to stop the pulling of muscle. As each section of muscle stopped burning, another would set aflame, sending convulsions up her body as she tried not to cry out. It was like nothing she had ever experienced before. As the spasms continued, the only thing she could think of was getting up and continuing to run.

She couldn't stay here long, but there was no way her body could carry her any further without resting. As the cramping slowly subsided, she pulled her legs back into the small opening in the ground and wrapped her arms around herself. With her body continuously vibrating, both from fear and weakness, she closed her eyes and tried to think of the one thing she wanted: home.

The snap of a tree branch, the rustle of leaves, and the thud of something hitting the ground not far from where she lay woke her. She noticed her breathing was heavy and tried to slow it, taking in each breath as deep as she could before releasing it and counting in her head.

The rustling stopped, and the woods were quiet again. The birds screaming through the trees had gone silent, and all she could hear again was the trickle of the water, slowly making its way through the pines. The vibrations of cramps had finally stopped, leaving behind an ache that covered the entire backside of her body.

She held out her hands in front of her to see how badly they were shaking, but all she could see was dirt and dried blood. A few of her fingernails were split down to the nail bed in her struggle to escape while two were completely missing, replaced by dark patches of scab-bing.

She closed her eyes and tried to listen for any sounds surrounding her, but nothing came. The dense fog had cleared from the ground, opening the woods up with cracks of light that came down in small rays. There was nowhere for her to run that wasn't out in the open. No darkness to cover her movements, to hide her, as she ran. The sun was just above her through the tree line and she knew that meant it had to be midday. She sank back into the hole in the Earth and decided that she would wait for nightfall before trying to move again.

She had to keep moving, she knew that. If she didn't move, she would be caught. If she was going to survive, and she planned on that, she was going to have to run again. Her body ached at the thought of having to stand.

It was going to hurt.

It was going to burn like hell.

But she wasn't going to die here.

No fucking way.

CHAPTER FIVE

EYVETTE

The motel room glowed a warm golden yellow as the sun started to bleed through the tattered curtains lining the wood-paneled windows. A small line of sunlight laid across my face and I could feel the warmth of its glow as I yawned myself awake. I had tossed and turned for hours last night, trying to fall asleep while thoughts of Charlie filled my head. Our childhood adventures seemed like such a long time ago, but being back here, even on the outskirts of town, brought back memories I hadn't been ready to process through.

The springs in the bed were protruding through the mattress and my lower back was numb from the pressure. I sat up and turned to face the window near the door. I stared into the rays of light coming in from just outside, each ray filled with swirling flecks of sparkling dust. The idea of having breathed in all those particles last night made my stomach turn. I put my feet on the ground, my socks pressing into the awful carpet. I had almost taken them off before getting into bed last night but decided it was probably best to keep them on. Not just to keep my feet from making actual contact with the flooring in the motel room, but also in case I needed to get my shoes on quickly.

My thoughts drifted from Charlie to the woods, then to the first of the missing girls, Meredith Bates. Every time I would get close to falling into a deep sleep, I would wake up from a nightmare of a woman, that I'd only seen in pictures, running for her life in the woods. I would try and shake it off, as best I could, before rolling over and trying to fall asleep again.

It wasn't as if anyone knew what actually happened to her, no trace of her had been picked up on. For all I knew, she could be in another country, living her life happily. The idea of her still lost out in the Pines didn't make sense to me and all the theories people had about her living life out in the woods, completely off the grid, didn't either. The woods were big, sure, but they weren't big enough that someone could stay hidden forever, not if they were living out there. I thought about how that would even work, living in the forest for the rest of your life. The fire you would need for cooking, the hunt for freshwater, and building yourself some kind of shelter.

No, she's not out there anymore and if she is...she isn't alive.

I knew that at least that much.

My thoughts shifted from Meredith to Charlie, as I got myself up and made my way to the small mildew-covered bathroom. The tile flooring was cracked and shaded with different-sized brown stains. The smell was indescribable but pungent. I looked into the mirror and worked my wide-toothed comb through my hair before gathering it up into a full ponytail puff.

This was it, the reason I came back here, to make my way out into the Pines and look for any signs of her. I would take the main trail that started on the edge of town and work my way into the forest toward the first, of many, stopping spots.

Charlie had promised me that I would love it here and, for a small amount of time, I found some joy being out in nature. We would stop along the trail just long enough for her to point out certain trees and rock formations, telling me about their histories. The main trail worked its way in curves up the state towards the North Carolina state line, with only a few lookout areas for people to stop and camp if necessary.

The first day of the hike would be the hardest, trying to maneuver through the thick brush that would try and grow over the trails. I would have to walk as far as I could, just to get into the open woods, where the pines grew in perfect lines.

I brushed my teeth, and took a few deep breaths, preparing myself for the start of what was going to be a long day of walking. I grabbed my backpack and re-checked all of the compartments, making sure that I had absolutely everything I could possibly need for the hike. I fumbled through the zippers to locate my small voice recorder, two flashlights, and the small knife Izzy had purchased for me to bring.

As skeptical as she was about me coming out here alone, she understood why I was doing it. Just like she would lose and gain weight for specific roles she got, she knew that the podcast was the only thing keeping me happy right now, and if that meant "going out into the woods to look for some white girl," then so be it. If I was going, I wasn't going "empty-handed". I appreciated the gesture, and honestly, it did make me feel better to know that they were there if I absolutely needed them.

However, the closer my flight date got the more unhappy she became. Then less than a week before my trip, the arguing started. But I understood it.

I checked my water bottle and made sure I had my small hand pump for more fresh water if I needed it. I zipped the small zipper back and threw the pack over my shoulder. As I opened the door, the familiar smell of fall hit my nose. It was a cooler morning here, the sun giving just enough light to keep it from being chilly.

I looked down at my boots, thinking back to the first time Charlie bought them for me.

"You're gonna need these," she said, her face full of excitement.

"Oh, no. Not these," I responded. I grabbed them from her, examining every inch of the boots. They were light brown, with fur-like material lining the edges, and sparkly purple laces zig-zagging their way up the front of each boot. "Charlie, why on God's green Earth would you get these?"

"They're very you," she said, letting out a deep laugh.

I shook my head, a laugh escaping me. I tried them on, at her request, still shaking my head in disapproval.

"They will grow on you, I promise. Besides, you'll need them next weekend!" she reminded me. "Gotta wear them a bit to break them in."

"Break them in?" I asked, still looking down at the boots.

"Yes! You can't take new boots out in the woods, you'll get blisters. Need to wear them a few times and make sure they're formed to your feet."

"Great," I said, rolling my eyes at her.

"Oh hush, they'll come in handy when we are hiking, trust me."

The purple laces were darker now, still sparkly in some spots, but covered in dirt and mud from the last hike I had taken almost five years ago. It felt like a lifetime ago since I stepped foot in this town, Charlie being the only reason I stayed as long as I did. I took a deep breath and walked across the gravel lot toward town.

It was one of those places you'd see in a movie, where no matter how much time and progression happened all over the world, it stayed exactly the same. The old storefronts even hadn't changed, their signs rusting and fading into the buildings.

Growing up here was exactly what you think it would be like for a young, queer, mixed girl in South Carolina. If people weren't busy minding my business outright, they would talk amongst themselves when I would walk in somewhere, ducking in towards each other and using their hands to cover the words coming from their mouths.

I learned at a young age that it was better to stay focused on myself, rather than trying to change anyone's mind. The church ladies in town would walk far enough around me on the sidewalk that there was no way for me to think it was accidental. The passive aggression built as I got older and, when Charlie and I started hanging out, we were the talk of the town. But it wasn't until her Mother started to hate me that it got to the point of us not being able to be in public together.

People, who had never spoken to me as a child, now felt it their responsibility to tell me all the ways I was going to hell and how I was ruining Charlie's life. They didn't realize that it was her that had come to me, that she had let me know how she always thought I was beautiful. I never thought it was anything serious until she invited me to go hiking with her. She was always in the woods and even though she had joked about taking me camping in the Pines, I always shrugged it off.

The moment she handed me the boots and told me I needed them for the following weekend, I knew it was more than just some childhood crush for her. As horrible as it was here sometimes, it still felt like home. The familiar feeling of knowing exactly where you were, knowing that most people there would never change, yet now knowing who you were in comparison.

I followed the sidewalk that led up the road from the motel, crossing a small bridge lined with train tracks no longer in service, and straight through the heart of town. There weren't a lot of people out this early in the morning, but the smell of fresh coffee was making its way down the street from the only coffee shop within 30 miles. I stopped, pushing the glass door inward enough to allow me and my pack through the doorway.

The moment the door closed behind me, the bell attached to the top of the glass frame chimed, causing everyone in the shop to turn in my direction. I pursed my lips and gave a half smile, nodding my head to somehow let them know I was from here without having to say a word. Everyone turned back to their newspapers, their morning coffee dates, and their half-eaten breakfasts. I could feel the surge of anxiety slowly dissipating as I turned toward the counter.

Standing next to the front register, leaning over the bar towards the young barista, who looked all of 17, stood a man that I recognized almost immediately. His face looked exactly how I remembered it on the fliers and news interviews that were circulating online. Clinton Bates, here in the flesh. Standing in the town his wife had gone missing from only mere months ago.

I swallowed hard, remembering the one small interaction I had with him only a month ago. I wondered if he would recognize me, the voice on the phone asking him questions regarding his wife's last whereabouts, and what her life was like leading up to her disappearance.

He turned his head towards me as I approached the counter and, from the look on his face dropping to an almost frown, I imagined he knew exactly who I was. His face seemed a bit sharper around the edges in person while his interviews never made him seem as unbelievably tall as he is. Something about him always seemed a bit too eager to me, interviews filled with hopeful words to a wife he hoped was somewhere out there listening to him.

I stopped just a few feet away from him, pretending to not notice who he was, hoping the barista would turn her attention towards my coffee order.

"Eyvette Thompson. Now, what are you doing here?" His voice was deep and I was unable to read the expression on his face.

I didn't know whether he was asking sarcastically, or if he had figured out why I would be in this small town.

"Mr. Bates?" I asked, trying to sound thrown off by having run into him randomly.

"The one and only," he replied, lips curling up towards his high-rising cheekbones. "What brings you to Travelers Rest?"

"I was raised here," I said, dodging his question with something true. I shot a smile back toward him. Our first and only conversation hadn't been awful, but he wasn't happy that I was asking questions about Meredith.

"I'm aware," he started to tell me. "I did my research, just like you." His smile didn't change. It was almost like he was telling himself to remember to keep smiling.

It didn't sit right with me, but, after a year of working in a business involved in true crime, I was always skeptical of the husband.

"Good," I told him. "It's always good to know who you're dealing with." The flirtatious way in which I said it slipped out, almost making me shiver in disgust with myself. I continued to smile, then turned my attention to the young barista. I wasn't going to let him know that just standing in front of him gave me the creeps.

"So, what are you doing here?" he asked me as I took my final step toward the register.

"Getting a cup of coffee," I answered him. His nostrils flared a small amount, and I could see the smile on his face trying not to shift. *Fuck*, I thought to myself, but maybe talking to him here in person would be good. *I need to back off of the sarcasm and secretive talk then maybe he'll open up a bit more.* "Then I'm heading out to the trails to start hiking."

His eyes widened and the smile on his face grew a half-inch.

"It is a gorgeous day for a hike," he said. "Are you here alone?" His question turned my stomach over in my body and I let out a half laugh from the anxiety it gave me.

"Yeah, I've hiked out here alone plenty of times," I lied to him. There was no way in hell I was going to let him know that the idea of being out in the Pines alone was terrifying to the point I'd changed my mind multiple times.

"That's awesome," he told me. "I'm actually going out today to look a little more myself."

"Oh?" I began, trying not to sound too desperate for information. "Any news or updates recently?" I knew the answer already, but, at this point, I wasn't aware of how much he thought I knew and maybe he had a bit of insider information from being such a big part of the search.

"Nothing major," he said, his lips turning into a straight line as he bobbed his head in an up-and-down motion. "I just keep coming out here and looking again, hoping that something stands out, you know?"

I nodded my head with an understanding look on my face. It had taken me over a year, but I felt like I was finally getting the hang of putting myself on someone's level when talking to them. It felt almost manipulative, but I learned that faking genuine concern often led to an easier conversation filled with more details.

"I feel like at this point, everyone has just given up. And now with that *Ellis girl* having gone missing, all the attention has gone to her," he said. "You knew her, didn't you?"

I tried to stop the twinge I felt from him mentioning Charlie's name from spreading to my face. He had obviously seen the threads online talking about our connection after "researching" me. My phone call had triggered something in him, acutely aware of how reporters get their information.

"Yeah, a long time ago," I answered him, shaking my head.

"And you're just here to go hiking, hm?" he asked me again, his face tilting to the side.

There wasn't a point in lying to him now. He knew why I was here, which meant he knew exactly why I had called him for information regarding the disappearance of his wife.

"Look, I'm just doing what I think is right," I started to explain to him. "We knew each other a long time ago when I still lived here," I said, my hands waving around to point out the town. "We used to go hiking out here, so I thought I'd check places we used to go."

"So, you're what? Investigating?" he asked him, the smile returning to his face.

I could feel the deep breath pushing itself out of my body as I started to answer him, reminding myself to smile and be nice.

"Wouldn't call it that," I said to him. "I'm searching."

"Searching?" he responded. "Searching for what?"

"I don't know. Guess anything that shows me she was out here. Answers maybe," I told him.

"Well, I'm hiking in from the North trail this afternoon if you want some company," he said, handing me a small card with his cell phone number and email on it. "I've got a few more stops to make, but I'm going to hike as far as I can before sundown." The front of the card was embossed with a small square picture of his wife with the red school bandana, just like in her missing posters.

I grabbed it and turned towards the counter again. I nodded my head in his direction, raising my hand with his card in it, and ordered my coffee to go. I didn't plan on teaming up with anyone and I wasn't interested in his company.

The moment I was back outside, I slipped his card into my back pocket and continued my walk through town. The Northern opening of the trail Clinton had mentioned was the exact entrance I planned on hiking in from. I didn't like the idea of being out in the Pines with him trailing not far behind and made a mental note to hike a bit further than originally planned. If I could make it past the first checkpoint then I could find a small opening to pitch my small tent and camp for the night.

I reached into the side of my pack and grabbed my phone. Now was my only chance to check my emails, and voicemails, and maybe send a text before my reception went out. There were no missed text messages and the only voicemail was from yesterday when Penelope called me for a third time just to "check in."

I hadn't answered her last two calls and planned on lying to her after this trip. Maybe I'd tell her I started my hike early so she wouldn't know I was avoiding her calls. I wasn't exactly happy with the way things had gone down at home before I left and, I'm pretty sure, Izzy was just as disappointed with her.

I continued my walk through town, finishing off my cup of coffee as I reached the last brick building on the street. Across the road, the sheriff was getting into his car. He was young and, like most of the cops in this town, had taken over for their fathers, and their father's fathers.

My last run-in with him had been less than pleasant.

Sheriff Andrew Burke, oldest son of the former Sheriff Burke who had been "let go" from the police department after a scandal involving drinking and driving and an underage girl found with him at the time. After dodging a plethora of phone calls from me, he finally answered and refused to speak to me.

He knew who I was, and I remembered him vividly, having gone to the same high school I attended. He was an asshole then, and not much had changed over the years. He was tall, with a muscular build, and had scruffy facial hair covering most of the lower half of his face.

He answered the phone and snapped almost immediately after I introduced myself. He didn't want anyone asking him questions, especially not someone he considered an outsider. He reminded me that this was a nice and quiet town and the Sheriff's department could handle these disappearances themselves. That I should go home and focus on my life, not poke around here for answers he could find on his own.

I tossed the empty cup into one of the small, metal garbage cans that lined the side of the road in small tourist towns. I kept an eye on him as he slipped into his car then took off in the opposite direction. I wondered if he had received my email that I was, in fact, coming to town and that I would make sure to directly quote him on my podcast.

The sun was still rising, but the streets hadn't yet filled with the swarms of bikers, hikers, and outdoorsmen. If I was lucky, I'd be the only one on the trail this early and could avoid any potential run-ins with people of my past, or any backpackers that might even recognize me.

CHAPTER SIX

GIRL IN THE PINES

Her eyes flew open, hands reaching to her sides on instinct. Another nightmare. Another reminder that she still wasn't safe, not yet. She blinked rapidly, trying to get her eyes to adjust to the fall of night encircling her.

The soft purple of the sky was fading below the treeline and Cicadas began to sing in a chorus of noise that raised the hairs on the back of her neckline. Her legs were sore and stiff to the touch. The spasms and cramps had finally passed, but left behind muscles that desperately needed time to heal. The cuts covering her body had scabbed over again while the dirt and mud dried to her like a second skin.

Reality began to set back in as she examined her body, checking her wounds to make sure none were bleeding. It was time to run again. As she moved the branches and rope-like vines from in front of her, she crawled forward toward the trickling of water. She used it to wash her face, which felt so unbelievably dry, then scooped it up and pressed her cupped hands to her lips. It didn't matter if the water wasn't clean, it didn't matter if it would hurt her stomach, she was too thirsty to care at this point. She took a few big gulps of water and then lifted herself up to stand. She turned in circles, squinting her eyes in an attempt to see as far into the woods as she could. The singing of insects around her made her stomach turn, but there were no other sounds coming from the trees around her.

She turned back to the left and began to follow the water that ran through the woods. Getting turned around in the Pines wasn't difficult to do and, with all the chaos from the night before, she didn't know exactly which way would lead her out of this hell. *The water had to run somewhere.* So she was going to follow it as far as she could.

As she started to run, she did her best to avoid the branches and dry leaves that had fallen, making sure that she made little to no noise as her feet hit the ground. Hoping to hear any sound that came from around her, she took each and every stride as carefully as she could.

The Cicada songs that assaulted her from every direction were starting to fade around her as her mind started to replay the events that led her to this very moment.

She had run, just like she had told her to...

She slipped herself from under the small crate she was hiding behind and ran, cutting the bottoms of her feet as she pushed herself across the rotting wooden floor. Her body slammed into the doorframe, throwing her back towards the ground. The chains that lined the door were thicker than her fingers and, as she pulled on them, she felt the weight of each and every link.

The flashes of memories were blurring in her mind, the fear in her body trying to wipe them from existence. The things that she had seen, all the screams that now echoed around her, the blood.

So much blood.

The muscles in her legs were trying their best to carry her, but her energy was draining with every single movement. The ground was starting to get harder now. The bank of trickling water grew, the stream of water following its every motion. She pushed her way through the small brush that grew around the base of the trees and found herself running between two dense rows of pines. The opening grew until the leaves and sticks between her turned to dirt. She stopped for a moment, pressing into one of the trees to her right and ducking down to look around.

The lines of trees surrounding her gave limitless options of openings, the trails led off in every direction, each in a perfect line. She tried to catch her breath, looking down each trail for any signs of an exit out of the woods.

It was too dark, she knew that. She was going to have to make a decision and stick with it. One of these paths could lead her out of here, that was true, but that same path could also lead her further into the Pines. No matter which direction she chose, she would have to keep moving.

Her mind kept replaying the previous night, throwing image after image at her: Blood pooling on the floor underneath the girl hanging from the ceiling...Heavy steps from the large person who walked right past her hiding spot. Large black boots covered in mud. The terror she felt as the screams came from another room just beyond her.

Her stomach turned inside of her, making her lean to the side with nausea. The guilt she felt after leaving her there still lingered, knowing there was nothing she could have done to save her. She had been so afraid, she still was, and she listened when she was told to run.

What else was she supposed to do?

Chapter Seven

Eyvette

The gravel road leading into the parking area showed no cars left behind from early morning hikers and families camping not far from the trailhead. The silence that surrounded the entrance into the forest was eerie, not even leaves rustled in the fall morning. The gravel under my feet was loose, creating the only source of noise, as I walked towards the opening of the trees before me.

Charlie's face flashed before me as I entered under the canopy of pines, smiling wide with teeth peeking out from under her upper lip.

This was the last place I saw her years ago; at the end of a weekend camping trip ending in an emotional shouting match in the gravel lot. The days before had started normally, the two of us singing along to our favorite songs as we walked into the woods, prepared for a weekend of cuddling near a campfire and escaping the people in town.

I remember being nervous to tell her about moving to Los Angeles. She knew it was always a dream of mine, but I hadn't told her I had spent the last few months saving up all of my money from work, searching for apartments near the city.

We weren't officially dating, nor had we ever really talked about what we were or could be in the future, we were just enjoying each other's company. We were so young back then. None of it mattered to me. I had to escape this town and I expressed that to her more than once, but I also knew how happy she was here.

She found comfort in the outdoor side of things here in South Carolina, seeking happiness within the woods by going camping and hiking, and, generally, spending most of her days outside. I grew to enjoy those things alongside her too, but I couldn't see a future where I was happy in this place.

It was bad enough that everyone looked at me like an outsider, even though I was born and raised here. The melanin of my skin and the texture of my hair didn't fit within the confines of what this town deemed "normal". It was different for her, easier.

Charlie was the literal apple of this town's eye, fitting the mold of what a small, white country town saw as perfection. The prom queen who doubled as head cheerleader and student body president. While I was just the light-skinned Black girl she befriended.

I agreed to go camping that weekend because I knew it was the only time I would be able to get her alone and tell her I couldn't stay in this place any longer.

I stepped into the shadow of the treeline and pulled down on the straps of my pack. I shook off the memories of her, reminding myself that it wasn't smart to go into the woods without a clear head. I wasn't afraid of being alone out here, but I was always someone who was capable of getting lost in my thoughts if I wasn't too careful.

Getting lost out here was easy, something Charlie told me over and over again. She would tell me the best way to get lost was to walk without paying attention, often pointing out trees and landmarks that would guide us as we made our way out of the woods at the end of a weekend.

Something I quickly learned over the last year of taking deep dives into people's personal lives with the podcast was simple: always leave breadcrumbs to find your way out if you get in too deep.

That same rule applied out here.

It was cooler in the woods than in town, the temperature dropping almost immediately after stepping inside the lines of tall pines that encircled you. It didn't take long before you were unable to see the start of the path you entered. The trails here were mostly dirt, the grass and vines beaten down along the path from years of hiker's and camper's boots.

I searched along the bottoms of the treelines as I walked, hoping for some small monument of days past, something that could help lead me in the right direction. My plan was to make as much headway from the trailhead as I could before stopping to pitch the small tent I carried.

As I walked, the mental checklist of all of my supplies filled the quiet inside my head, making notes to personally remember why I had packed each item.

A small tent that could barely fit two adults.

A heavy flashlight, that I could feel on my right side, inside the small pocket of my pack.

Matches.

A small tube used to pump fresh water.

A box of shitty power bars that didn't require the use of fire or water to eat.

A small pocket knife.

It would take me four full days to walk from the trail-head here, in Travelers Rest, to the top of the foothills that led into the mountains of Western North Carolina. Four days alone on the trail, with my thoughts, to check the locations Charlie and I visited when we were younger. There were three spots she liked to frequent on our trips into the Pines, claiming them as her "favorite" spots.

The first of the three was a large gathering of rocks that formed a small cave sitting on the edge of a lookout point roughly 15 miles into the trail. That would be my first stopping point and the first place I would search from top to bottom, looking for any indication that she had been there.

Weeks had gone by since her disappearance and the weather had turned from warm to cool, sending rain storms and foggy mornings throughout the Southern states. It wasn't that I knew what I was looking for, or if any physical clues would even exist after all this time, but I knew Charlie. If she was in trouble then she would have found a way to leave a trail.

The rows of pines began to narrow further as I made my way deeper into the forest, the brush around the base of the trees growing thicker and darker in color. Through the tops of the trees, I could make out blue and gray swirls of color, with just enough light coming through the canopy to light certain areas of the ground ahead of me. The cool breeze that made its way down the lines of trees made the thinner tops of the pines sway from right to left, bringing the woods alive around me.

I tried to keep my mind on the trail before me, mentally marking the rocks and large rotting stumps I passed as reminders of where I came from. My thoughts drifted from the woods to Izzy, probably still in bed back in our LA apartment, the sun not even rising yet. Our last conversation had been nothing short of crappy, her anger getting the best of her on the way to drop me off at the airport. My constant reassurance that everything would be fine wasn't enough to keep her from worrying or being upset that I was on the hunt for someone that I had once been with.

"I don't understand why this is so important to you, Eyvette!" Izzy shouted, her hair bouncing around as she tilted her head to the side, shooting me a look across the car.

"Oh, we're going full-on legal names, are we Isabella?" I snapped back, pursing my lips together and raising my eyebrows. I knew how this went with her, when she pulled out my government name, all bets were off. "You're the one who pushed me into doing this podcast in the first place!" I continued on as she turned her head away from me. "Remember?"

"Hell no, I do *not* remember that! I remember *you* wanting something to fill your time with and letting Penelope talk you into this shit," she said. Her jawline was tight and, I could tell, nothing I said was going to pull her out of it. But that didn't stop me from laying it on thick. I wasn't about to let her have the last word. Not involving something I was doing to ensure I could keep up with her.

"Right, because what I do and how I make money isn't important to you? You'd rather me just be the girlfriend who follows you around and lets you pay for our existence, right? Is that what you want?" I turned my body towards hers and stared at the side of her face. "Want me to just stay some broke-ass girl from South Carolina you swooped in and rescued from a little coffee shop?" I took a deep breath, stopping myself from going any further. Her eyes shut for a moment before she turned back towards me. *I went too far...*

"Yeah, Yvee, that's what I want. I want you to resent me for making something of myself and loving you," she said, voice calmer than I had anticipated.

"That isn't what I meant and you know," I started before she interrupted my train of thought.

"Oh, yes it is. Don't worry, you've made it abundantly clear that I'm the issue here. You know what I think, Yvee?" She crossed her arms across her chest and sat back shaking her head. I stared at her, my eyebrows raising, waiting for the answer. "I think you're constantly in some bullshit internal competition where you think I'm competing with you. You somehow think that *I* think I'm better than you because of dumb luck!" she continued to shake her head, eyes starting to well with tears. "I refuse to let you turn this into some holier-than-thou bullshit quest."

"What? I'm doing this because it'll be good for the podcast, good for you and me, not to make myself feel better, Izzy," I assured her. She just continued to shake her head, unable to look in my direction. "Charlie is just someone from my past, you know that. There's no hidden agenda here, Izzy, I swear. I wouldn't be going if it weren't for the podcast."

"Fuck the podcast!" she snapped, eyes finally making their way in my direction. "What does it even matter? You can keep doing what you've been doing!"

I pulled my head back, shooting a confused look her way.

"Fuck the podcast? Izzy, this podcast is the only career I have right now. It's the only thing that's worked. But it's getting bogged down by all that legal bullshit. I need something different, something bigger. That's what this entire trip was supposed to be about," I told her.

"Yeah, I hear you," she said back while looking out the window of the car.

"Can you stop being so mad at me about it then, please?" I asked her.

"It isn't just the podcast, Yvee. It's all this bullshit. Charlene's missing, so are two other girls, and you–what? Do you think you're different from them? That you're untouchable?" She questioned, tears in her eyes starting to fall down the side of her cheeks. "You know, I don't care what you do for work. I never did. But this? This idea of walking into the woods in some backwoods-ass town to look for someone who probably doesn't even want to be found? That's stupid, Yvee. It's so fucking stupid." She wiped her face with her hands and turned to face me. "You know I love you...and you know I support you in whatever you do –but this? This shit, right here? This shit is dumb," she said coldly.

"Well, guess I'll just have to be dumb. Not all of us get to play make-believe with our famous friends for money," I snapped at her, knowing that it was a kill shot.

"Right," she said as the driver pulled the car to the curbside of the airport. "Have a great flight."

"Izzy..."

"Just get out, Yvee. Go do your bullshit," she said, looking away from me and the airport behind me.

"I'll text you when I land," I told her. I leaned over and kissed her right shoulder. "I promise everything will be fine. I'll be home before you know it. I love you." I stepped out of the car and barely had time to close the door before the driver pulled off.

A small pile of rocks and some stacked wood lying on the right side of the trail brought me out of my memories just as quickly as I had fallen into them.

The ground burned in a perfect circle, grass black and dying in a ring around it. Someone was here recently, judging by the small amount of smoke still sifting its way through the cracks in the stacked rocks. A campfire for someone to get themselves warm, but still burning this early in the day? There was no sign of a tent having been here, no trash, or other signs of a camper being anywhere nearby. *Odd place to start a fire.*

Charlene would always tell me to walk off of the trail, preferably into a dense part of the woods, until I could find an opening big enough to pitch a tent and make a fire that wouldn't harm any of the other trees hanging over.

Whoever built this fire wasn't an avid camper, nor did they know the unspoken, but common sense, rules of campfires within the woods.

I scanned the trail around me, turning myself in a full circle, peering between the tall trees that surrounded the edge of the trail. I gripped the straps of my bag, and pulled them downward, tightening the pack to my back. I knew I wasn't alone in the woods, no one ever was, but there was something unnerving about the unmanned fire that made me start walking faster.

After a few hours of walking, the trail opening and narrowing throughout certain parts of the forest, I was starting to feel a slight incline. I knew I was making good time and getting closer to the site of the cave. The path was beginning to change from mostly dirt to scattered rock. Every step of the trail brought more memories of a life that seemed so far from me now. The trees, the smell of pine, the crisp air; it was the same as I remembered.

I had just made it to another widening part of the trail when I heard a snap from behind me. It almost sounded like a thick branch getting split in two over someone's knee.

I stopped and threw my body around in quick motion, but all that I could see was the narrow trail I had just passed through, the trees swaying in the wind. *Maybe a fallen branch*, I thought, reassuring myself that the noise in the woods was more than normal. The wildlife and the weather were all capable of making strange sounds.

I laughed to myself, reminded of Izzy's comment about a Black girl alone in the woods. As I turned back towards the opened trail, I caught a glimpse of the sky above me through the break in the treetops. Dark clouds loomed over the part of the forest I was standing in and the wind had picked up ever so slightly, bringing with it a roll of thunder and storm clouds. *Fuck.* The weather was always iffy here in South Carolina, but I hadn't prepared too heavily for a storm. Hopefully, I could stay ahead of it and set up camp as close to the rock cave as I could get. With the wind pulling wisps of hair out from the hair tie and the pine needles in the vicinity circling me, I decided to push on.

Chapter Eight

Girl in The Pines

The rows of pines stretched farther than she could see in all directions. The dense forest behind her felt like a wall, pushing her towards one of the paths. If she set off in the wrong direction she could end up circling back and there was no way in hell she was going back there.

It played like a movie in her head...the bloody pool on the floor...the screams echoing all around her...

She closed her eyes and leaned into the tree next to her, body folding down toward the ground. She was so tired, still in so much pain from the cuts and wounds covering her body. The cuts on the right side of her face started to sting from tears she hadn't even noticed falling. She wiped them away with the remaining right sleeve of her denim shirt, not caring about the blood stains all over it, like some twisted version of tie-dye.

The only thing her mind could do right now was remember...and she couldn't stop the memories from flooding in around her.

The pool of blood made its way across the floor toward her hiding spot, following the cracks in the old and broken hardwood. She clasped one hand to her mouth, the other pushing herself further into the dark of her hiding spot. She didn't know how long she had been under the small bed-like structure in the corner, hands shaking while she tried her hardest not to breathe.

She had watched countless horror movies, remembering her constant comments about how those girls in the film couldn't keep quiet enough to not get caught. It wasn't until this very moment that she truly realized how hard it was. She pressed her hand harder into her mouth and bit down between her thumb and pointer finger, trying everything to keep herself from screaming.

She had thrown herself under the bed just as footsteps made their way across the floor from outside the front door. She had tried over and over again to undo the chains wrapped around the girl hanging in the front room, her body covered in stab wounds. Her hands were so shaky she couldn't get a grip on anything and, by the time she thought to search around the small shack for anything to break the chains, the sounds of someone approaching caught their attention.

Screams erupted from the back room, but all she could focus on were the chains wrapped around the girl's body.

"You have to go! You have to run!" The girl whispered quickly. "Please!"

"I can't just leave you here," she countered, hands pressed to the bloodied face, still shaking.

"Go!"

She closed her eyes for just a moment then turned around. The sounds outside the door were starting to get closer. She noticed sheets hanging over the floor, just off the side of what looked like a bed, and she dove for the floor, pieces of wood splintering off into her palms. She hit the ground and rolled to the right, just in time for the door to swing open. Pulling her knees into her chest, she bit her lips and tried to control her breathing. Her whole body was shaking as the large boots stepped past her.

The girl in the chains was trying as calmly as she could to talk herself out of the situation, while someone continued to scream from beyond the other door in the room. She wished she would just be quiet, just let whoever they were come in and go. She could get them out of here, she just needed time.

She tried to calm her breathing and just feel the tree she was leaning into, feeling the hard ground underneath her. She couldn't stay here, she wasn't safe. She looked straight ahead, decided on the center path that made its way through the long line of tall pines, and stood up.

The silence in this part of the forest set her thoughts on fire, but she knew that she had to keep going. The muscles in her legs were starting to cramp again and, if she didn't run, they would give out on her and leave her helpless in the middle of the woods. She gripped the tree and steadied herself, ready to take her first steps into the path, when the sound of moving air wisped behind her.

Before she could register what was happening, she saw it.

Just behind her head, only a few inches above, it was lodged into the tree–an arrow. She turned her head quickly in the other direction, falling back towards the tree, just as another arrow hit the tree to her left.

Her breathing increased and her body started to react without her permission. Before she knew it, she was on her feet, running straight into the line of trees to her right.

It wasn't the path she picked, not consciously, but her body was in full flight mode and it was her only option.

As she made her way past another row of trees, she cut to the left and took off into the next row of trees. But just before she slipped into the line of pines, something hit her right shoulder, throwing her to the right as she ran.

She caught herself mid-scream, throwing her hand over her mouth, refusing to allow the rest of it out of her throat. The burning in her shoulder was radiating down her arm as she kept running, ducking into another row of trees before pushing herself into a full sprint. Refusing to look as she ran, she felt something warm running down the right side of her back. As she weaved in and out of the pine trees she caught a glimpse of something reddish-blue staining her denim shirt. As her shirt now stuck to her body, she knew–it was blood. Panic rose up in her anew, forcing her body to move even faster.

There was no right or wrong direction, just alive or dead. Right now, she was alive, and the only way to stay that way was to run.

CHAPTER NINE

EYVETTE

The thunder roared around me, shaking the trail I was walking on.

Thunderstorms always sounded so different in the woods. It couldn't echo off of buildings and structures, or be dampened by a comforter pulled all the way over my head. It was loud, like the crashing of ocean waves against the shore, like a train running its way through the intersections of a small town. It was almost tangible here in the forest, the ground sending vibrations up my entire body while I pushed on through the incline ahead of me. I had always loved a good storm, especially when it came out of nowhere on a cool, fall day.

My only concern, which kept me from enjoying the commotion around me, was that I was still a ways off from the cave where I planned to set up my tent. The last thing I needed was to be trapped out here without any shelter so my plans would need to change.

But thunderstorms always made me think of Izzy, the only other person in the world who possibly loved them more than I did.

Growing up in South Carolina, storms became a regular occurrence. During the summer, like clockwork, they would roll in late afternoon and dump heavy rain around the town. While most kids stayed inside, not daring to venture outside in the rain, I gladly took the reprieve from the people who inhabited this wasteland. Thunderstorms meant that I would have the entire town to myself and I took full advantage of it whenever I could.

Izzy always told me how different the storms were out in LA. She would explain that it wasn't like they were for me back home.

So, we took every chance we got while we were in another city for some press junket, or for her to film on location. We would pray for a good storm to come through and, often enough, one would roll in.

It always ended with a giant pile of snacks in the bed and one of her favorite movies playing. She would pull the curtains open and crack the window; letting the breeze and the loud crashes of thunder sweep through the room.

There wasn't much that didn't remind me of her and, out here in the woods, the only thing I could think about was how badly I had hurt her feelings before leaving.

I promised I would check in and let her know that I was okay. I had, but, as expected, I didn't get any kind of response. I knew she was upset with me and she had a right to be.

I realized a long time ago that when I felt backed into a corner, I would aim for the jugular, saying the first thing that popped into my head when I was angry. I was capable of being mean and I knew that. It took me years to let go of all the hatred and vitriol spat at me growing up, only to find myself grown up and still angry. Izzy understood where I was coming from, but sometimes I pushed it too far when we argued.

I made a mental note to apologize to her when we were face to face again and explain how I never wanted to make her feel small.

The trees were swaying so quickly above me that I felt almost pushed forward by the wind. I realized quickly that this storm was coming in fast and I had no chance of outrunning it. I needed to find somewhere safe to pitch my tent and I needed to do it quickly.

The sun was no longer visible in the sky, and the woods around me becoming less vibrant and almost gray, making my visibility worse as the winds picked up.

I searched around the trail, looking in each direction for a clearing in the trees, somewhere that would protect me from the wind, but give me enough room to fit my tent. To my right, I noticed a small group of clustering trees. *An old campfire site?*

I steadied myself and pushed against the wind toward the place where I would set up camp. It looked as though someone had used this spot prior to me, the ground flattened, and a makeshift stone fire ring lying to the side of the opening. *Perfect, exactly what I need right now.* It was surrounded by large pines that rose from the ground in a circular motion around the campsite, providing extra protection from the wind.

I dropped my pack to the ground and pulled the liner of my tent out of the large straps that held it in. I heard a snap from behind me, much like the one I heard earlier when I was walking. I stopped, only for a moment, to look around while my hands continued to unroll the small tent.

Nothing, not that I could visibly see at least.

It didn't matter, I had to get this pitched before the rain started.

I tossed the tent like a fresh sheet over a bed and started to piece together the small rods that snapped together to create the posts that would hold up my shelter. I felt the cold drops of rain starting to hit the back of my neck as I slipped each pole into its place, lifting the roof of the tent off the ground. I had barely secured my canopy when the sky opened up, lightning striking a tree nearby while thunder seemed to come straight from above me. I tossed my pack into the tent first, crawled in, and zipped the liner behind me.

The wind sent the rain thrashing across the side walls of my little tent, my body weight the only thing holding it in place. I didn't have enough time to stake anything to the ground, though it wasn't likely the stakes would hold in the wet ground during this storm.

I sat with my legs crossed in front of me, the darkness slowly washing over me, as the storm finally made its big entrance on the other side of the vinyl tent flaps. I took my jacket off, rolling it up so rainwater wouldn't splash all over the ground inside the tent. I slipped my hiking boots off, placed them in the far corner, and readied myself for a long evening of thunder. I wasn't going anywhere tonight, not in this mess.

With a heavy sigh, I set to work on unraveling my puff from the hair tie. My hands worked automatically, one smoothing down the hair along my scalp while the other gathered it up to wring out the rainwater. Thankfully, I managed to escape not long after the downpour started. I didn't bring my usual array of hair care products, not wanting to overpack and weigh my bag down. After re-doing my hair, I decided to focus on the storm beyond my vinyl shelter.

The thunder roared overhead and a crack of lightning brightened the right side of my tent, making contact with a tree not far from me. I loved thunderstorms, truly, but I was realizing I loved them from the safety of a warm bed.

I loved them when I was with Izzy, the whole world of noise blocked out for just a quick thunderstorm break. This was nothing like that. Between the sound of the tent flaps slapping about and lightning bouncing off the pines around me, I wasn't feeling very safe at all.

I pulled my flashlight out, from the side of my pack, and placed it beside me. *There's no way I would have been able to outrun this storm*, I told myself, glad I ultimately decided to stop and make camp. I would hunker down here for the night and get an early start once the rain cleared. I laid myself back, using the bottom of my pack as a makeshift pillow, and I clasped my hands across my chest.

One night down and I was nowhere close to any an-swers.

Maybe this had all been a mistake after all...Maybe Izzy was right...this was a stupid idea... I shook the feeling of being wrong off, closed my eyes, and let my mind drift off while listening to the sounds of the thunderstorm.

The sound of branches snapping not far from the tent woke me. I sat up quickly, instinctively reaching for the flashlight beside me. I sat still, listening as best I could through the rain pelting down the side of the vinyl.

Another snap, this time closer than the last. It was coming from the right side of where I was. I slowly turned my body towards that side of my tent and raised the flashlight over my head. I hoped it was just the storm; knocking loose branches towards the ground or an animal on the hunt for shelter in the woods, just like I had.

"Hello! Is anyone out there?!"

The voice startled me to the point I clasped my hand over my mouth to stop a shriek. My eyes were wide as a few more branches snapped within only a few feet of my tent.

"Hello?" His voice was low, washed out by the rain, but I knew it was a man. A man in the middle of the woods, in the middle of the night, probably still on the trail not far from my tent. "Anyone? Hello?!"

I sat for a moment, my brain still trying to wake itself up, but before I realized what I was doing, I heard myself speak.

"Hello?" I called out through the vinyl tent flap, still holding onto my unlit flashlight. I closed my eyes and winced. *How stupid was I? What the hell was I thinking?*

Izzy's face ran through my mind, making that face she always made; head tilted to the side with her eyebrows raised in confusion, lips pursed together like she was deep in thought. I could hear her voice, clear as day, asking me if I was crazy. It was almost as if she was right here in the tent with me.

"Where are you?" the man's voice asked. "Hello?"

He wasn't far from my tent, but the darkness in these woods only allowed for about three feet of visibility. No lights for miles meant there was nothing to help you see the silhouettes of the trees and trails. Plus, with the storm overhead, there would be no light from the moon or stars either. It was pitch black outside.

Against my better judgment, I turned my flashlight on and directed it toward the sound of the voice outside my tent.

"I'm here," I said, flashlight shaking as I reached my other hand into my pack and pulled out the knife I was carrying with me. I gripped the handle in my hand as tightly as I could, eyes closing again at the thought of potentially having to use it. "I have a knife!" I followed up as loud as I could. I winced again, hearing just how terrified I sounded.

"I'm sorry, I'm not trying to scare you, I just got caught out here in this storm!" the man said, now closer to my tent.

I turned towards the zipped flap beside me, pointing my flashlight where I guessed he would be standing.

"I just don't know exactly where I am right now."

My fingers held the zipper's pull tab and moved it a few inches to the left, undoing the zipper teeth just enough to look outside with the flashlight. In my head, I kept reminding myself that anyone trying to hurt someone in the middle of the woods wouldn't announce themselves or let someone know they were there.

"Hello?" I said, peering through the small opening I created with my hands. "Who's out there?" I looked from left to right, moving my flashlight around, able to see only a few feet with the rain coming down so heavily. "Where are you?" I had barely gotten the words out of my mouth when his face came into view just to the right of my tent.

He was tall, his head covered by the hood of a rain jacket. He was leaning to the side, holding one hand up to block the beam of my flashlight, pointed directly into his eyes. His sharp features were unmistakable, his jawline as if it was purchased out of a fashion magazine. Clinton Bates, wearing the same outfit I had seen him in just this morning at the coffee shop in town. He was soaking wet, with just a small pack on his back.

"Eyvette?" he said, leaning further down to see my face through the small gap in the tent. He moved his head around, trying to get a better look around the beam of my flashlight.

"Mr. Bates, what are you doing out here?" I asked him, my body slowly relaxing behind my flashlight, the light finally stable on his face. He jerked back, moving his face out of the light's path. "Oh, sorry," I moved the flashlight beam toward his chest. "Are you okay?"

"Just wet and lost," he answered, "I tripped not far back and busted my flashlight." He waved a small black flashlight in front of him, the front plastic screen cracked and covered in mud. He stood there awkwardly for a moment, neither of us saying anything else before my brain finally connected the dots.

"Oh, shit, I'm so sorry, here," I said, realizing that I was still holding the knife up toward him. I turned, placing the knife down and pulling the zipper around the rest of the flap to open the front of my tent. I didn't know him, not personally, but it felt weird just leaving him standing alone in the storm. I pulled my pack from the corner and moved it to the right side of me, opening up a small amount of space on the ground next to me.

He put his hand up and pulled the flap, giving himself enough room to walk his way into the small tent before rezipping it closed. "Thank you," he said, putting his pack in the corner of the tent. "Fuck, it's so bad out here." He pulled his hood down and unzipped his jacket, working his arms out of it before balling it up and placing it on his bag.

"Yeah, I barely had time to get my tent up," I said, sliding myself as far to the right as I could. He was so tall, his body barely able to fit sitting upright in the tent. I watched him pull his knees up towards his chest, struggling to not take up any more room. "What are you doing out here?"

"I was trying to make my way up towards the main campsite by the caves," he told me. "What about you?" He was breathing heavily like he had been running.

"Are you sure you're okay?" I asked him again, my face unable to hide the questionable look I was giving him.

"Yeah," he said, giving out a little laugh. "Once my light went out, I got a little spooked." He wrapped his hands around his knees, the rest of his body still soaked from the rain. "I'm not a huge fan of the woods...and the darkness doesn't help," he said, his face looking almost embarrassed.

"Yeah, it's always been really dark out here, so when it storms it's almost impossible to see anything at all," I told him. "Anyone would be spooked." I gave him a half smile, hoping it would make him feel a little better.

"Thanks," he said. "I'm really sorry if I scared you. I was trying to get a little further up this incline before setting up my tent." He patted his pack, where a tent was rolled into the holder at the bottom. "I thought I could make it up, but once the lightning started, I realized I waited too long."

"Yeah, I made it in my tent just as the sky opened up. I figured I would get an early start tomorrow," I told him. I didn't know why I was telling him any of this or, better yet, why I was talking to him at all. The fact that I even let him into my tent was still swirling around in my head, mostly coated in Izzy's concerned voice. She would have let him stay out in the rain, no doubt in my mind. "Have you found anything at all?" I didn't know why my word vomit refused to stop, but I was always one to ask questions regardless of the situation.

"No, nothing worth mentioning," he said, leaning his head down in disappointment. "Sometimes, I wonder why I even bother to come up here."

I adjusted myself on the ground, looking toward him.

"What do you mean?" I asked him.

"I don't know...I've been doing this for months and I got nothing. No one will talk, nobody in town, not the police, no one." He unclasped his hands, moving them around while he spoke. "The people in this town don't want an outsider poking around. Hell, half of them probably think *I* murdered my wife," he snapped.

It startled me a little. I wasn't expecting him to take it there, but I did feel a twinge of guilt since I was one of the people who was on the fence about whether he was or wasn't involved in his wife's disappearance. "Listen, the people in this town have always been like this," I reassured him. "I hated it here, for that reason exactly. But that shouldn't stop you from looking for answers. As for the police force here, well, they're a joke, especially Sheriff Burke."

"I know...it hasn't stopped me, it just...it hasn't made it any easier. I know the cops aren't telling me something. All of this just doesn't make sense..." He paused, seeming to think for a moment before speaking again. "So, you know the Sheriff, Eyvette?"

My eyebrows raised up while I nodded my head 'yes', but my brain started to fire questions at me. "What do you mean? What do you think they know?" I asked him. "What makes you think that?"

He shifted in the tent, face lighting up at my questions as if he was excited to give me his perspective. "Listen, Meredith wasn't the first person to go missing here, not by a longshot," he told me. "Multiple people have gone missing from here, all the way up to the foothills." He reached into his pack and pulled out a small brown leather notebook adorned with a small symbol on the front of it.

I couldn't make out the exact design, only that it was a small, triangle-ish emblem pressed into the leather.

He opened the book and ruffled through a few pages before pointing it at me. It was a list of names, written in pencil, each with a date next to it. "All five of these people have gone missing within the last 10 years, all from different spots on the trail, none of them seen again. Some in the foothills further North, some right here in town."

I grabbed the notebook from him and pulled it towards me. "All of them?" I asked, reading through the list of names with my flashlight. I didn't recognize any of the people written down, nor had I heard about them. "How is that possible? I haven't heard of any of these people."

He grabbed it back from me and put it back in his bag. "Exactly! Most of the cases were closed, or the families reported a history of mental health issues. They just decided that these people were mentally unwell, and decided to disappear or walk off into the woods and kill themselves. It's fucking crazy."

"But there have been no sightings? No bodies?" I asked, my mind racing. "How is that possible? There was nothing on the news about them."

"Local stories were run, but nothing on any major networks. I started poking around and asking questions about the other missing people on this list, but people still refuse to talk about it."

"Where did they go missing?" I asked him, still in disbelief. "With that many disappearances, you'd think they would have a major case, right?"

"Well, that's just it, not all of them went missing from this area or even this town. There are well over two hundred miles of trails out here between South and North Carolina. So, since they weren't all from the same place, people didn't want to–or hell maybe they just refuse to see them as being related."

"That's fucking insane," I responded. "Do they have any connections?"

"None that I've been able to find. The police said they aren't connected since two of them are men and the people going missing here are women," he said, rolling his eyes. "Did you know it took more than three days for me to be able to file that Meredith was missing?"

My face went from confused to shocked.

"Are you serious?" I asked him.

"Yes! Was told that since she had gone camping with coworkers, she was probably still out here in the woods and decided to go off on her own. I was the *only* person out here searching for her for *three days*. Not even her parents were concerned until the police reported her as a missing person." His voice cracked a bit when talking about her parents. I hadn't thought about how they felt about him or if they were on his side or not.

"I'm sorry, that's awful, but there have to be answers out here somewhere," I reassured him.

"I mean, that's what you're doing here, right? Trying to find answers for your podcast?" He didn't look at me when he asked and I hoped he didn't notice my instinctual facial reaction.

It stung a bit, because it was true, and I was starting to feel guilty about it.

"Yeah, that was the original plan. I was supposed to come here and find Charlie, or find some kind of answer as to where she could have been," I told him, pulling my knees to my chest. "I know it sounds shitty."

"No, I didn't mean it like that, I know you two were close."

"Yeah, a long time ago... I don't know, it seemed like a good idea at the time I guess."

"I've listened to your podcast, you know?" he revealed, "You're really good at what you do, and I like that you do your research before telling a story. I'm sure you have just as good of a chance at getting to the bottom of this," he told me, smiling.

"Heh, yeah, maybe so," I chuckled. "I still can't believe this has been going on and no one has been able to do anything about it. Or, at least, no one has been willing to." *What has gotten into me?* I'm not sure why I felt so comfortable conversing with him; maybe because he was easy to talk to. "But, if I'm being honest, I gotta say I wasn't sure whether you were or weren't involved at first." I could tell this was something he was used to hearing now, judging by his reaction.

"I figured. Most people do, honestly," he told me, his head turning to hang downward. "I get it, really. I'd feel the same way about someone else's spouse too."

"Yeah. I guess I feel like if Charlie was just trying to disappear then she would have told *someone*. I can't stop thinking that she's probably just..." I stopped myself before I could finish the sentence, but Clinton's face turned towards me, suddenly looking sad.

"Dead?"

"Yeah." I heard myself responding.

He turned his face away, looking towards the other side of the tent flaps.

"I'm sorry, I didn't mean to sound..." my voice trailed off. I didn't know what else to say or if there was anything else to say.

"It's okay, really. I've felt that way a few times. You know, Meredith and I weren't perfect, but I just can't imagine her leaving me and not saying anything. We had our issues, sure, but I loved her."

I don't know why, but I believed him. He genuinely seemed concerned about Meredith. Why else would he keep coming out here? Why willingly put himself through all these hikes and all the bullshit from the authorities in this backwoods town? No reasonably sane person I could ever think of would do that.

I reached over and pulled out my phone from my pack. *2:45 a.m. If I'm going to hike in a few hours then I need to try and get more sleep.*

"Listen, I'm gonna try and sleep a little before getting up to hike. If you want, you can tag along with me, at least until we get to the caves. If you want?" I offered.

"That sounds good. Thanks again, you know? For letting me crash," he said, chuckling a little bit.

"No problem," I reassured him before turning around to lay against my pack again. I turned my flashlight off and, shaking Izzy's voice of anger out of my head, tried to drift off to sleep.

CHAPTER TEN

GIRL IN THE PINES

The tackiness of blood oozing down her right shoulder was the only thing she could focus on while weaving herself between rows of pines. She was running out of breath, air stinging her throat as it made its way to her lungs. She jumped through the row of trees to her right and turned back, just for a second, before she moved into a new row of trees.

Was no one there? *No, he was there, hiding.*

Was there really no one chasing or closing in on her as she ran? *Can't take that chance, keep going!*

How far had she run? *It doesn't matter, not safe, not yet!*

The blood from her shoulder worked down the ripped denim shirt, staining it darker. No feeling was left in her body as she ran. No tears formed. No pain held her back. Nothing hurt, not anymore. Neither her feet nor her muscles. The tendons that once struggled against her had yielded. They weren't pulling against her or struggling to stop her body from continuing on its forward momentum. There was nothing. Nothing but the empty feeling of knowing she wasn't safe.

She wasn't alone.

Someone was out here with her. It was the same person keeping the screaming girl in the old cabin she found. The same person the girl in chains was with. No, she wasn't alone out here, and she knew it.

The longer she ran, the more her mind started to slip into memories, no longer paying attention to each and every foot she threw forward in her run. The ground began to fade and the trees blurred into a haze. She was standing in the cabin, blood pooling around the floor under the girl in chains. The screaming from the other room was growing louder, more desperate, for someone to help them...

She left them...both of them...

She was told to run, but she decided she wasn't going to. She would stand up to whoever it was, but when the door to the other room opened and the woman screamed...she instead pushed herself out from under the bed and ran. She ran as fast as she could, turning back just as she pushed the door out, catching just a moment's glimpse of the open door behind her.

There he stood, tall and broad. A man, wearing all black from head to toe, towering over a girl screaming in the corner of the room. He turned to face the exit, hearing her feet on the rotting hardwood outside the front door. She could only barely make out his eyes through the black face covering.

The girl on the floor reached her hand out as she cried and begged for help, her body covered in what looked like dry blood.

The man turned and stood still, just watching, as she ran from the house.

The edge of the makeshift porch forced her attention off the man and back to her surroundings. Before she could catch herself, her knees and elbows made contact with the rock-covered ground surrounding this hellish cabin. She could feel the skin stretch and rip further as she forced her body up, ignoring the sting, and forward into the woods. She stopped for a moment in the treeline to look back.

She left her to die...She left them both to die.

She cried into her hands, covering her face to try and muffle the sobs bellowing out of her. She could barely see with the tears stinging her eyes as she pushed her way further into the darkness of the Pines. She ran until her legs gave out, cramps starting to run up the back of her body, leaving her immobile on the forest floor. She pulled herself over to a large overturned tree and pressed into it. The blood from her knees and elbows started to dry, and the cold night air wrapped itself around her.

She untied the denim overshirt wrapped around her waist, threw it over her shoulders, and slid her arms into the sleeves. Her body vibrated, fear working its way through her bloodstream, as she tried to catch her breath. Barely able to keep her eyes open, but the sound of a branch snapping from behind her sent panic through her entire body anew.

Before she had a chance to move, hands were around her neck, yanking her out of the safety of the fallen tree. Her head and shoulders made abrupt contact with the tree behind her, hard enough to make her see spots. The soles of her shoes scraped against the bark as the hand forced her neck harder into the pine, silencing her screams.

She kicked her legs off the trunk as hard as she could, loosened bark falling against his boots, and pressed her foot into him with all of her weight against the tree. She felt a burning sensation in the right side of her body, as he slid a knife alongside her with his other hand, opening her skin. She continued to kick as he slit lines across her stomach and chest, slashing back and forth across her body with the knife. She couldn't breathe, and she was having a hard time keeping her eyes open.

His eyes were wide and had an almost dead-like quality to them, and he watched every wince she made. Without thinking, she lifted her hands and slammed them down on either side of his neck as hard as she could. Her pinky fingers and wrist throbbed as they made contact with his collarbones, but he didn't react beyond an annoyed growl. She had no other means of trying to break free; she lifted her hands again, but this time aimed at his eyes.

Her left thumb slipped into his black facemask enough to connect with his eye, pushing as hard as she could, while her other hand clawed at any exposed skin between the mask and his collar. As she pushed, he pulled back, swinging the knife aimlessly towards her while letting go of her throat with his other hand. She kicked once more, as hard as she could muster, and shoved herself off of the tree towards him. She pushed her thumb as far as it would go, finally letting out a guttural scream that was held within. He stumbled back, just a few steps, as she fell to the ground. She greedily pulled in as much air as her body would allow, before forcing herself up and into a run. It didn't matter what direction, it didn't matter how far or how long, she just needed to run. She jumped over the fallen tree and took off in a full sprint deeper into the forest.

She wouldn't stop, not again. She would run as far as she could and pray to any God listening that he wouldn't follow.

The branches and thorns that arose from the ground cut into her exposed legs, pulling her toward the Earth as she ran into the darkness. They snagged and ripped through her denim shirt, allowing the foliage to slice across her skin.

Her body burned then, just as it did now, but those cuts were no longer fresh and sticking to her shirt.

The memory of the attack faded as the trees around her came back into focus. Her shoulder still burned, but it didn't matter, none of it mattered anymore. She had to keep running. It was her only option now.

CHAPTER ELEVEN

EYVETTE

"Hey," he greeted me as I sat up in the tent. It took me a moment to remember that just hours ago he was wandering around outside of my tent in the storm. "It looks like the rain has finally stopped." The front of the tent was half unzipped, letting the cool morning air drift in, the smell of pine gathering inside the tent.

I turned to face him, examining his face in the daylight, in an attempt to put together all the pieces of who he was and why he was here. "Yeah, looks like it," I yawned, covering my mouth and letting out a laugh after. "Sorry, I'm so tired. We should probably get moving though."

He nodded and pushed his way forward, exiting the tent.

It didn't take long to collapse the tent, rolling it up and strapping it to the bottom of my pack. I gathered up the rest of my things, pulling a small power bar from my pack and throwing the bag over my shoulder. I stood up, sliding the wrapper off the power bar, taking a bite while looking around my impromptu campsite. Setting up camp in the middle of a storm had me slightly disoriented, but after getting my bearings, I turned to my new hiking buddy. Clinton finished pulling the straps on his bag tighter before giving me a nod that he was ready to head back out into the forest.

We walked the narrow trail at the same pace. It was still slightly overcast outside, the sun slipping in and out of the clouds that hung above the treeline. We only took small moments to stop and look along the side of the trail if we noticed someone had recently been there. I wasn't sure what we were looking for and, after all the rain, the odds of finding anything other than fresh tracks were near impossible.

Clinton talked randomly about his other trips into the Pines, telling me about all the people he had encountered while out hiking. It was mostly families of young campers, couples on weekend getaways, and the occasional professional backpacker making their way back home. He wasn't suspicious of any of them, nor would I have been in passing on a trail. That was pretty normal in this area and, the more I thought about it, the more I realized that the trails had been relatively empty during this hike.

"So, what are you expecting to find up here at the rocks?" Clinton asked, turning to face me so he was now walking backward.

"Not really sure I'm expecting to find anything, honestly. With all the rain this season, I don't know what there'd be left to find. Guess I'm just hoping to see something that lets me know she was here, you know?" I absently pulled the straps of my pack and shook my head, pushing off the thought that she was gone. Charlene was an avid hiker. She knew what she was doing out in the woods and wouldn't just walk away from her entire life. That much I knew for certain, but proving it? That was going to be difficult.

"I get it. I do," he said, shaking his head back at me. "I feel like if Meredith really wanted to leave me, she would have just done it." I felt my lips pulling wider, my face starting to express an awkward expression. "What," he questioned, "do you not think so?"

"Sorry, no," I smiled weakly at him. "I didn't mean anything by it. Obviously, *I* don't know your wife, so I can't say what she would and wouldn't do. Only you can." I raised my eyebrows at him, trying to let him know that I truly wasn't trying to be rude. "I believe people leave for all kinds of reasons. People run away all the time, right?"

"Yeah, I guess so," he said softly, turning away from me and continuing on the trail.

"Fuck, Clinton, I'm sorry, I really didn't mean anything by it. I just–I mean that maybe she's still out there, just...I don't know, living a different life, maybe?"

"Do you actually believe that?" He didn't bother turning to face me as we walked side by side.

"Do you want the truth?" I asked, fully ready for him to say no.

"Yes," he said, stopping in his tracks.

I barely noticed, stopping a few steps ahead of him before turning around. "No, I don't. I don't think *any* of them just walked away."

We stood there for a second, staring at each other, neither of us saying another word. He shook his head, his face towards the ground, and let out a small cough into his closed fist.

We walked for another hour or so before the small cave of rocks started to grow in the distance. I was almost relieved at the sight of it, ready to sit down for a moment and gather my thoughts. Clinton threw his bag down and started to explore the outside of the cave, running his hands along the stone sides. I followed him, looking from the top to the bottom of the rocks, and remembered all the prior times I had been here.

It was exactly the same. Trees growing out from the cracks in the rocks, stones scattered with moss, and rock-carved names that people had vandalized the place with. There were no signs that anyone had made camp around the cave, nor was there any leftover burnt wood from a fire. The ground seemed untouched, almost like no one came to visit anymore. I made my way inside the North opening of the cave and pulled my flashlight out of my side pocket. I could see inside without it, but it would allow me to check the tops and sides of the cave walls.

The stones opened up to form an almost perfect square roughly the size of a studio apartment in Los Angeles. The ground was solidly packed with brown dirt, greenery beaten down by cavegoers over the last few decades. This place was one of the first that Charlie took me to on our first camping weekend together. It didn't seem as magical to me now, but the memories were all good. I turned my flashlight towards the walls and started making my way around, uncovering the same markings that had been here forever. Amongst the stones in the middle of the room were two sets of initials, marked off by a giant heart. I remembered the moment immediately. Charlie had begged me to snap a Polaroid of her with our newly etched names in stone. I shook my head, not needing to dwell on the past memory, and continued on around the cave.

There was nothing here, not that I expected anything really. Thankfully, this wasn't the only place within the vicinity that I wanted to check. There was a spot just off the trail side of the cave where a little pool of water formed in the creek that ran downhill. It was the first place that Charlie kissed me, after splashing freezing water over us both by jumping into the small pool.

I made my way out of the cave, shaking my head in disappointment towards Clinton, who was now sitting next to his pack eating some kind of granola bar. He shrugged his shoulders and continued eating as I walked toward the thick trees beside the cave.

"Where're you headed?" His mouth was full, granola spilling out into his hand.

"Gonna just look around. Plus, I gotta pee," I said, pointing toward the woods in front of me. "I won't go too far."

I walked into the tree line, using my hand to push branches of small pine trees aside. I pulled pine needles out of my hair as I walked further in, trying to watch the ground around me. The forest grew more dense with each step I took, and after a few more branches swinging towards me, I pushed through the final bit of brush and stood in an open area.

A small stream trickled down the side of the foothills, gathering into a circular shaped pond, before pouring out the other side and continuing down the incline. The ground was moist around me so I made sure to place each step carefully, watching the ground for small holes that water ran beneath. Once I had my footing, I stopped and gazed around the water.

It was bigger than I remembered, but probably still just as cold as it had always been. It was probably the best memory I had from my last trip here with Charlie. The water was freezing, having run down from the top of the mountains. It didn't matter what time of year it was, it never warmed up.

I remembered the feeling of pins and needles across my skin when I finally worked up the nerve to enter the pool with her. This was the trip I was dreading so much. The trip where I would tell her that I would be leaving South Carolina. I wasn't sure why I waited to do it here, but it just felt like the right time; away from town, with no one around to judge us. The moment those words slipped out of me, her face sank. Her eyebrows pushed in toward each other and her eyes began to well with tears. I tried to explain all the reasons this place was bad for me, what drove me to this decision: the hateful people, the racist remarks, the constant nagging about how I was ruining THE Charlene Ellis just by existing. She never said a word, just grabbed her sweatshirt, pulled it over her wet body, and picked up her pack. We didn't speak until we reached the head of the trail, just a few feet from the gravel parking lot we parked in. I had broken her, I knew it.

Days turned into weeks then months into years. The silence between us never truly broke. Then, once Izzy entered the picture, my memories of Charlie began to morph into something that resembled friendship, especially when compared to the love I had now.

I realized, only then, that it wasn't just the town I was running from, but her.

Water swirled around in the circular pool, the rocks that lined its outer sides were soaked and black. I had barely taken a second step before I noticed it. There, sitting under a small overturned tree, barely visible unless you were walking around the pond, was a small backpack. I watched the ground as I stepped from rock to rock, trying my best to keep my balance, but also keep my eye on the pack across the pond. Someone had been here, that was certain, but were they still around?

"Hello? Is someone there?" I yelled in the direction of the backpack, hoping that if someone were near, they wouldn't be startled. My thoughts suddenly went from finding someone to someone, instead, finding *me*. I shook the thought as I made my way around the far side of the water, no one answering me.

The moment I reached the bag I noticed how wet it was. *It's been here for some time.* I noted as chunks of the ground came up with the pack when I lifted it. For how long I didn't know, but I could guesstimate, from the way dirt had gathered around the bottom and the water stains, that it was out here during a few storms.

I opened the top strap, pulling the drawstring out of the loop, to reveal the largest compartment of the pack. There wasn't much in it. Just a few items of clothing, a water bottle, and a small notebook. I sifted through the clothing and found a few shirts that, I imagined, belonged to a female. They were mostly dirty, small, graphic tees. I pulled each one out, examining the fronts and backs carefully. Once I had them laid out beside me in a pile, I reached further into the bag to pull out the small leather-bound notebook.

It was simple and leather bound, with no actual design on it, but had a small, leather rope tied around it. It looked similar to the one Clinton carried with him but smaller. I untied it, gingerly, and opened to the first page. The page layout resembled a diary, the script not completely filling the space, and was dated from about half a year ago. The first few pages were mostly short stories, retelling the author's outings with friends and navigating through anxiety. A lot of lines were small notes about wanting to manifest happiness.

I turned through each page, reading through, almost embarrassed for the person who left it there. I was going through someone's personal thoughts and almost felt bad about it. After coming across a few smeared pages, probably from the water, I flipped to a page that caught my attention.

The words were written in black pen ink, like the rest of the pages, but what drew me in was the handwriting. It wasn't the same as the rest of the journal. It was more bubble-like, letters swooping in what looked like circles. I stared at the page before me and traced the words with my fingers as I read:

You don't have to keep doing this to yourself.

He isn't good for you, Mere.

I meant what I said, we could leave and no one would ever know.

I can't stand the thought of you going home to him, getting tossed around and yelled at.

If what we have is real, we should try and figure it out, right?

These trips are getting harder and harder the more we do it.

I'm sorry for leaving so early, but your friends are right, it isn't fair to involve other people in our mess. They care about you, so I understand. I'm sure one day they will like me.

This is easier than saying goodbye with everyone around.

Miss you already. Think about what I said.

Love, Charlie

"Charlie...What the hell is this?" I asked myself, pulling the journal closer to my face as if it was going to tell me what was going on. I read through the words again, stopping on the bottom line. Charlie, out here with a woman who was obviously having an affair with her. "Mere?" I mused, my gaze going from the book in my hand to the pack on the ground. I closed the leatherbound notebook and slipped it into my jacket pocket, turning toward the bag. I pulled another shirt from it and opened it up like the last few I removed. This wasn't a shirt, no, it was a large red square, detailed with a diamond in the center, and a school mascot directly in the middle of it.

A bandana.

This wasn't just any bandana. It was the same one I had seen in pictures plastered across news stations and blogs. The same photo that was used on social media in the "Girl Missing" flyers.

This pack belonged to Meredith Bates.

Mere...the letter was written to Mere–Meredith.

I placed my hand to my mouth, my head shaking back and forth naturally. *How–How was this possible?*

Did they know each other?

They were friends?

More than friends?

They were here. Charlie was here!

I stood up, bandana tight in my hand as I turned in circles to look out around the pond. Silence was the only thing with me here. My mind exploded with questions, thousands of them rapidly firing at once. I tried to grapple with the idea that somehow the two of them had met, started seeing each other, and then met out here in the woods. *Meredith had been camping with friends though*, I thought to myself. No one had said anything about Charlie being part of the group. That would have been pertinent information since both of them had gone missing.

My thoughts continued to scatter around me before finally taking me back to Clinton Bates, the man still waiting for me back at the base of the caves. The words in that letter to Meredith were clear. *"Tossed around and yelled at."* Clinton Bates was abusing his wife. The media had skirted around the subject but never had any physical proof. After all, getting physical proof was hard when your wife was missing.

I stuffed the bandana back in the pack, covering it with the shirts that lay all around on the forest floor from my rummaging. I zipped it up and placed it back near the fallen tree, before stepping back to gather my thoughts.

Was Clinton Bates dangerous?

Did he know about his wife's affair with Charlie?

Was that why he was eager to hike together back in town?

Was that storm the perfect cover to end up here with me?

Searching for Charlie?

For Meredith?

A long shiver made its way up my spine, forcing me to take a deep breath and close my eyes. Izzy would be freaking the fuck out right now. Her brain was a constant cesspool of true crime shows and murder mysteries. I shook her out of my head for a moment, attempting to process all the questions I was asking and answering for myself.

I was out here in the middle of the woods, alone, with Clinton Bates, husband to a missing wife, who was having an affair with Charlene Ellis.

Fuck! That was the only thing I could keep repeating inside my head.

Izzy was right, this was stupid, and I was stupid.

My prior opinion on whether or not I believed Clinton Bates had, or had not, been involved in his wife's disappearance had changed. This new information changed everything I thought I once knew. He had hiked up here for weeks, searching for any clues that led to his wife, starting with the caves. He specifically told me his wife had no reason to leave him, but, to be honest, I took that with a grain of salt. Most people had no clue who their partners truly were and, after a year of delving into people's personal lives, I knew that most people had secrets. Secrets they even kept from their closest friends and family.

I stood there, just staring at the pack on the ground. With a hand on my hip and the other still covering my mouth in disbelief. What the *fuck* was I going to do with this? The thought came and went as a voice sounded from behind me.

"You okay?"

I whirled around and jumped back, letting out a small scream. It took my brain a moment to process that the voice belonged to Clinton. He, also startled by my scream, jumped back a step.

"Whoa! I'm sorry, I didn't mean to scare you," he said, letting out a half laugh. "When you didn't come back, I thought you may have gotten lost."

I stood there, feet frozen to the ground, while internally telling my face to look normal. "Oh, yeah, sorry. I... I was searching around a bit," I said, trying to force a smile onto my face. "I came across this place," I lifted my hand and circled it around, showing him the small pond.

He noticed the bag almost immediately, eyes widening and lips parting. "Holy shit!" he exclaimed, proceeding to jump from rock to rock and making a beeline towards the pack on the ground. "This is her pack! This is Meredith's pack!" He hurried past me, slipping on the rocks and nearly falling to the ground as he got closer to the fallen tree the bag lay beside. "Did you see this?!"

It felt like my rib cage had constricted around my lungs, making it harder to breathe. I mentally debated the words I wanted to use before responding. "Yeah, I... I just saw it when you scared me," I lied, turning towards him as he leaned over to lift the pack off the ground.

"Fuck, it's soaking wet!" he fussed, lifting the mud-covered bottom of the bag with his hands. "I can't believe this!"

"How do you know it's hers?" I asked, playing up the fact that I hadn't looked through it.

"I know because I gave it to her," he answered, almost sounding snippy, and turned the bag around to show me the back of it. "Look," he rubbed his hand along the bottom flap of the bag, swiping away the mud to uncover a small rectangle made of leather. The letters "*MB*" were etched into the small rectangle. I nodded my head in understanding. He started to sift through the bag, pulling out the same shirts I had just placed back in.

How close had he been to seeing me with it?

He continued through the pack, unaware of my internal panic, and finally pulled out her red bandana with the school logo on the front of it.

"What is it?" I asked, trying to sound as sincere as possible.

"She wore this when she backpacked," he answered, clutching it as tightly as he could in his hand. "She was here... This had been here the whole time–how did I miss it?" He grasped the edges of the bag's compartment and turned it, shaking the remaining contents onto the ground.

He was hunting for something. I could tell. I tried to look over his shoulder as best I could, before asking another question. "What are you looking for?"

"Uh... nothing really," he began to gather up the clothes he had pulled from inside and he almost looked...dejected, "Just... seeing what all is here."

His answer made me question whether or not he was telling the truth. My hand unconsciously slipped into my jacket pocket and felt the seam of the leatherbound notebook. He was looking for the journal, I knew he was.

"She always carried stuff to write on.." He checked the two front pockets and pulled out a small black pen. "See? Here's her pen, but there's nothing else."

I gripped the notebook in my pocket tighter, taking an instinctive step back, at his observation.

He moved through the rest of the small pockets, pulling out a red flashlight, a granola bar, and a small black box. He opened it and immediately placed a hand to his mouth, his body still.

"What's wrong?" I peered around him, looking over his shoulder as I questioned him. He lifted the object up over his head, letting out a shaky breath. In the small box, he was holding, sat a small diamond-cut gold ring. "Is that," I started to ask before he interrupted me.

"It's a ring," he muttered, taking a big breath in. His face snapped towards me, cheeks warming from emotion. What that emotion was, I wasn't sure.

"Maybe she took it off while she was hiking?" I offered, my face tensing up as I said it.

"It isn't hers," he replied monotonously, lowering his hand and the box back to his lap.

"What do you mean?"."The *ring*," he snapped, "This isn't *her* ring." He was visibly angry now, his face flushed red with fury. At first, I thought he might have been upset to the point of tears, but no. This was genuine rage.

"Well, whose ring is it?"

"I have no *fucking* clue!" he shot back at me, flinging the small box into the pack and zipping it up angrily. He stood and moved to walk away, almost stepping directly into me before stopping and catching me off balance. "I'm sorry, I'm just confused, that's all." He continued to walk in the direction we both had come from.

"It's alright," I reassured him, moving out of his path before cautiously following.

I looked back where the bag once lay and, once more, let my hand feel the journal's edging. At that moment I knew I would have to break away from Clinton Bates. Something didn't sit right with me.

That ring in Meredith's bag...who had it belonged to? Anyone else who found a ring would immediately think something weird was going on, right? I think I would... He was searching for the notebook, but for what? Maybe he knew she was seeing someone? Maybe he knew she and Charlie were spending time together?

The uneasy feeling inside me grew with each question I tried to answer. But a single question still swirled in my mind and, no matter how much I wanted to, I still couldn't answer it:

Was I safe?

Chapter Twelve

Girl in The Pines

The trees grew in all directions the farther she ran. Her body no longer hurt and the blood on her had dried, making her skin feel tight. The only thing she felt was the cold air entering her lungs, stinging like ice with every breath.

It felt like she had been running for hours. She didn't stop for the cramps that had both returned then vanished, nor the pain in her shoulder that had now gone numb.

No. There was no stopping.

Not now or ever.

The forest floor no longer sent painful vibrations from her feet up through her legs. Her legs were now stiff and solid, like the trunks of the fresh pines, after being eclipsed by pain and muscle spasms.

None of it hurt her anymore.

All she could think of was getting out of this never-ending forest. There was no telling what direction she was running. No way to know if she was any closer to freedom than she was yesterday. The day had slipped away, the sky turning purple above her as darkness crept through the base of the pines. She wouldn't be able to run once darkness settled in around her, not out here. She would have to walk, carefully feeling her way through the woods. She could not stop, no matter how tired she felt. Her skin was so dry, and she was thirsty.

As she slowed her run into a walk, her body began to feel again. All the trauma to her body was pulsing, sending her heartbeat throughout her body. She felt it everywhere, comforting her. If her blood was pumping, it meant her heart was working, and if that was true, then she was alive. That was all that mattered right now.

The sky above swirled dark purple and gray clouds around, the sun slipping down just beyond the tree line, where no orange showed in the sky. It was beautiful. The Pines were full of beautiful things. Even the darkness brought its own form of beauty. Owls screeched while cicadas sang so loud that they formed a symphony that shook the ground. It was so loud sometimes, then so silent the next moment.

A part of her just wanted to give up. Just lay down and never move again. To stay here and change seasons with the Pines, buried by the Earth over time. Her body would give out, and within a few years, people who knew and loved her would forget her name. She would become a memory that occasionally drifted through someone's mind throughout their life. She imagined the ground opening up and swallowing her, taking away all her pain, and then the snow would eventually start to fall. Her body would lay there, untouched by humans, yet explored by nature until it was no more.

That thought alone didn't scare her, but the reality of surviving this horror did.

She would have to rebuild her life, spending her days remembering how she ran away. Her mind would re-member how she did nothing to stop what was happen-ing. Not by choice, no, but because her body had taken over.

Fight, Flight, or Fear. Those were the options that everyone eventually got. She always imagined that she was a fighter. Her entire life, she believed that she would stand up for anyone and anything that needed her. But here, in the Pines, she took flight. Fear enveloped her, filling her body with the only reaction it could muster.

She ran.

She stopped only for a moment to look back as the girl reached her hand out from the back room and cried out to her.

She left her.

She left them both to die.

They were dead, and it was her fault.

If she died, no one would know what happened to them. If she died, no one would ever know the truth. Their stories would die with them. If she died, they would all disappear into the forest, never heard from again. The feelings came and went, her memories of her life and family pushing the idea from her head.

She would not die here, no fucking way. She would not allow this to be the end of her story! No way in hell would she let someone take her down like this. She came here for a reason. Even though she knew she was leaving the

Pines alone, forever scarred by her time here, she was determined to exist.

To survive.

Chapter Thirteen
Eyvette

W e walked together in silence, the wind through the trees providing the only sound apart from our boots on the ground. Clinton stayed a decent length ahead of me, but I could hear him breathing heavily. My stomach felt full of stones, my anxiety building with every footstep. I fought the urge to run in the opposite direction, putting as much distance between the two of us as I could. However, my brain was sifting through the last page of the notebook, going over the words repeatedly.

I needed to know what Clinton Bates knew. I would be able to tell if he was lying to me. I just needed to ask the right questions.

Izzy's voice resounded internally between my scattered thoughts like a broken record. I could see her, head tilted to the side and eyes wide with panic, screaming at me: "*Run, bitch!*" Before I could stop myself, I laughed at the thought of it, causing Clinton to stop and turn toward me.

"What's so funny?" he asked me, his expression mixed between anger and confusion.

"Oh, sorry," I started, "kinda spaced out and remembered something my girlfriend said before the trip." I lied.

I would never tell him how my entire body wanted me to run away from him.

His face relaxed a bit, and he turned, settling into a stride right beside me. "Chambers, right?" he asked. "That's her name?"

"Izzy," I said. "She just goes by Izzy." The thought of her yelling at me was still circulating in my head.

"What's it like? Dating a celebrity?" He laughed a little and grabbed the straps of his pack as he kept walking.

"Uh, it has its moments, for sure," I told him. "But it's mostly great."

"Does she listen to your podcast?"

His question caught me off guard, and I hesitated before I responded.

"She listens, not sure she's heard all of it, but she supports me."

"And what does she think about you being out here, looking for another girl?" My face twisted into a look of discomfort, something he noticed before I could respond. "Shit, sorry, Eyvette, I shouldn't have asked. Not my business."

I relaxed for a minute, taking a deep breath while we continued walking. "It's fine, honestly," I told him, "She's not happy about it, I can tell you that much."

His following silence was loud, and I knew that the only way I would be able to bring up his missing wife was to continue giving him bits of information about my personal life. I grew more comfortable with this over the last year. In exchange for giving people small bits of myself, they would tell their stories in return. Doing this sometimes felt wrong, manipulative, and aggressive, but it always ended with the story I needed. "She didn't think it was a great idea for me to come back here."

"Why? Did she not like that you were looking for Charlie?"

Hearing him say her name so casually was odd.

"It's not just that. I mean, sure, that has a little to do with it, but she was more concerned that I was coming back here, to South Carolina," I told him.

His face started to show his confusion again.

"She didn't want you coming home?" he asked, letting out a sound of exacerbation like he was appalled by what I had said.

I looked at him, my eyebrows raised again. This was a common problem I had when talking to white people about coming home. Their experiences never matched mine in this town, let alone the entire state. I took a deep breath and tried to explain it to him without any underlying attitude.

"Look, it's different here for you and me," I told him, motioning my hands around as I spoke. "Sure, people here don't want to talk to you, you're an 'outsider'," I explained, making air quotes with my hands, "But, they can ignore you *and* be cordial. They don't call you names or make nasty faces at you, right?"

He shook his head, still looking confused.

"Okay, so... for me, people ignore me out of hatred–out of ignorance. You get ignored for asking questions as a stranger, but I spent my entire life being ignored by the town for the color of my skin." The lightbulb clicked in his head, and he immediately understood what I was trying to explain. Our situations weren't similar, never had been, and never would be. "Izzy knows this and was worried about me returning while people go missing."

He didn't speak for a moment, and I wondered if I had offended him, not that it would change how I would have responded to him.

"Well, that definitely makes sense," he finally said. "She's worried about you."

I nodded my head yes in agreement. It was time for me to turn this conversation toward him. "Did you and your wife come here a lot?"

He swallowed hard enough for me to hear, then answered.

"No, not really. I'd never been here before she went missing. She always had a good group of teacher friends from back home. One of them suggested taking a weekend away to Travelers Rest, and she fell in love with it," he told me.

Only one part of his answer made sense to me: "fell in love". Meredith had come here, somehow met Charlie, and had some torrid affair that led her back into the Pines.

"Do you know her friends well?" I asked him, trying to sound as casual as possible. The last thing I needed was for him to suspect that I was interrogating him for information.

"Not really," he said. "I had met them before in passing at school events, but Meredith kept her friendships to herself. She didn't ever go out or spend a lot of time away. Rarely did she have time off to come up here."

"So, why keep coming back?" I asked. "There are plenty of places to hike in Tennessee, right?"

His face twinged, and his eyebrows ever so slightly furrowed before he answered.

"I guess so. I guess she just liked it here. The cops asked me the same thing here in town," he said shortly. I could tell the question had hurt him a little, but I wouldn't stop. Before I could ask my next question, he continued on after his answer. "They were told she was going through a hard time."

"Who? Who said that?"

"The cops," he clarified, shaking his head, "Guess her friends told them that she was going through some things and she was trying to figure some stuff out. I asked them what and who said it, but they wouldn't go any further with it."

"Have you spoken to her friends?" I asked.

"Tried to...No one will talk about it. No one will talk about *her*."

"Why?" I wondered, "That's weird, right?"

"I guess so," he sighed, continuing to hike without making eye contact.

Something was off. He never mentioned this before, not to me or during countless media interviews. "Why didn't you ever talk about it? Why not go to the police about the friends?" I asked him.

"For what," he seethed, voice rising, "their help?" He laughed.

I could tell that he was starting to get upset, but that's what I needed. I needed him to talk emotionally. I needed to know he was telling me the truth.

"I mean, if her friends won't talk to you about her, there must be some reason, right?" I knew the question would bother him, but I continued, "Surely they would have told you if something was wrong."

He stopped walking and turned towards me.

"What're you asking, Eyvette? If I know why my wife got up and ran away?" His face wasn't angry like it had been earlier, but concerned, as if he was worried about my opinion of him. I shook my head no.

"That's not what I meant," I lied, placing my hands on my hips. "Just think it's odd her friends are acting so fucking weird. Like, maybe they know more than they're saying, that's all." I relaxed my face and tried to give a small smile. I could visibly see him calming down after I answered him. He was finally beginning to trust me. *Now I just need more information from him...and I know he has it.*

"Yeah, it's weird, you're right," he finally agreed, shooting me a half-smile.

"Do you have any theories about it at all? Any clue on what they could be hiding about it?"

He started to shake his head and turned to walk again.

"Yeah, I have some, but none that make any real sense, honestly."

"Try me," I said, turning to walk alongside him. I nudged him with my arm, playfully letting him know he could tell me anything. The questions in my head were piling on, but I needed to be careful in how, when, and why I asked specific things.

I was going to have to lead him into every conversation, making him believe it was actually his idea to talk about it.

Before going through with my plan, I reached into my back pocket and pressed the circular record button on my small voice recorder. Until this moment in the hike, I had forgotten I even packed it. But with him talking so freely, and Charlie still lost, I needed to keep as much recorded as possible.

He started rambling about how he never really knew Meredith's friends, but how she always talked about them, and how they were good people to be around. He explained that over the last year, she had come down to South Carolina over six times to go backpacking with them. He never really questioned her about it until that last trip.

Something was "off" about her sudden need to get away. But I let him ramble, going through the times he spent at the school where she taught, making appearances at events, and generally just being involved in her daily life. The more he talked, the more he went into details about the day she was finally reported missing. He told me, once again, that the police had been little to no help in the investigation and constantly questioned his whereabouts, which had been back in Tennessee, according to him.

After what seemed like hours, the sun began to dip between the tops of the trees and the sky, and the darkness started to spread around the forest floor. We walked until the sun was barely visible, then decided to jump off of the side of the trail and set up camp for the night.

This time, Clinton would be sleeping in his own tent, spaced roughly over five feet from the vinyl front flaps of my own. It left just enough space between us to start a small fire and rest from the day's hike.

I placed my pack on the ground inside my tent, quickly slipping the notebook out of my jacket pocket and into the front zipper compartment. I pulled the small recorder from my back pocket and placed it in the mesh netting hanging from the wall of my tent. I could keep it there and have it record all the conversations we had between our tents for the evening.

I sat and watched as he put his tent together, slower than I had, wondering how many times he had been here in the Pines. How many times had he put the tent up on these trails at night looking for his missing wife?

"What do you think she was doing out by that pond?" I asked, breaking the silence, as he snapped his tent poles into the ground.

"What?" he asked while fighting with the rods of the tent in an attempt to snap them into place.

"Why do you think her bag was by the pond?" I clarified for him. "Did she ever mention that place before?" He kept building his tent but took his time before answering me.

"No, she never mentioned anything about it. I knew she had seen the caves before. Showed me all kinds of pictures when she came home from her first weekend getaway."

"What about the ring?" I asked, pulling my knees towards me so half my body was inside the tent, my feet still on the dirt outside.

"What about it?" he grunted, still finagling with his tent posts.

"What was she doing with a random ring out in the middle of the woods?"

His last pole snapped into place, and he threw his pack into the tent. He took a second, crawled in, and then turned to face me.

"I have no clue," he answered sharply. He didn't seem angry, but I could tell he wasn't interested in discussing the ring further.

"Just odd, ya know? Maybe you should tell the cops you found her bag. Maybe they could start the search from there? Bring some tracking dogs out? Maybe they could pick up a scent from where she was."

"Yeah, well guess when we have service again I can call them and let them know where exactly it was." He pulled his jacket off and slid closer to the outside of his tent. "Speaking of, how did you know about the pond?"

I felt my chest getting tight and tried to fake a smile and think before answering him.

"Charlie showed it to me before," I answered honestly, noticing a slight flaring of his nostrils at the mention of her name. "She took me to the caves my first time camping out here," I told him, lifting my hands and pointing around us at the trees. "It was freezing cold," I laughed.

"So, you two were really close then?"

My smile started to slip away, but I held it in place while I responded.

"Yeah, we were...for a while. After I left we didn't really talk much," I explained.

"Did you love her?"

My expression changed, unable to hold that fake smile. The question seemed so abrupt, but sharing was the name of the game right now. I took a deep breath and let out a long-winded sigh.

"I think love is a pretty strong word. We were close when we were younger. I'm not sure I knew what love was until I was out of this place for a while," I told him. "We wanted different things, ya know? We were kids."

"Was she upset that you left?" He asked, rummaging around in his bag, pulling out another power bar of some sort.

"I think she was sad about it, but it was what was best for me. I was suffocating here." I hadn't planned on going further into detail about my history with Charlie, but if it meant getting him to open up about the possibility of knowing more about Meredith's disappearance, I would go with it for now.

"Was it really that bad?" he asked, sounding genuinely troubled by my past experiences here.

"It was pretty bad. It was hard enough not fitting into the town's ideals, but being the lesbian ruining the golden girl didn't help." I found myself explaining before I could stop myself.

Fuck, I immediately regretted the last part of that, *too much information.*

"Wait, so no one knew she was gay before you? They mentioned it on the news, and I saw it on a few of the posts some organizations created. Was it some secret?" His question was pretty on brand for a typical, straight, white man.

Didn't expect anything less, I thought and let out a small laugh.

"I mean, people knew, but once her family realized that people were talking about it...well, that was the beginning of the end. Her dad definitely wasn't happy about it, then I think her mom just kind of followed suit, I guess," I responded.

He shook his head in disbelief as if it were unimaginable that people in a small southern town could both be homophobic and racist.

"That's bullshit," he said. "I'm sorry."

I nodded toward him, then brushed past it, hoping to shift the conversation back to Meredith.

"It is what it is, ya know?" He nodded back, shrugging his shoulders in response. "She was out here in the woods all the time. To her, this place was the safest place she could possibly be. Away from all the people in town, alone with her own thoughts. She practically lived out here." Before I could stop myself, my questions fumbled in my head, and I let one slip. "Did they know each other?" I quickly forced a cough and reached for my water bottle, turning toward my tent and acting as if it wasn't a question I had been imagining since finding the notebook.

"What?" he asked after a short pause. "Did who know each other?"

I took a second to take a sip of water before responding, hoping that it made it seem like the question was completely innocent.

"Meredith," I explained, "I wonder if she happened to ever come across Charlie out here on one of her backpacking weekends." He scrunched up his nose and cocked his head to the side, shooting me a weird look. "What? Is that so hard to imagine?"

He let out a small laugh before responding, likely choosing his words carefully.

"I mean, it's not unheard of I guess, but she never mentioned knowing her. Plus, Charlene Ellis went missing weeks after she did." He was looking down towards the ground when he spoke, which felt strange since he had been talking directly at me before Charlie was mentioned.

I made a mental note of it and pressed on with a follow-up question.

"I just wonder if there was some connection between them? Maybe they were friends too?" I relaxed my legs, letting my knees slide from my chest to the ground in front of me, stretching my arms out towards my feet.

"Doubt it," he snapped back shortly.

I could tell the idea alone was bothersome to him, but I couldn't stop myself at this point. Both the ring and the fact that I knew about their connection wouldn't let me stop.

"So, what were you looking for in her bag earlier?" I asked him. "You said she wrote a lot? What about?"

His eyes were still looking towards the ground, face pulled into a strange expression, when he responded.

"Mostly notes, things she wanted in life, dreams–I don't know! I wasn't really looking for anything, just kind of hoping for some sort of clue. This is the first sign of her I've gotten in over *a month*, and it's frustrating."

"Why would you be frustrated? Isn't the bag a good sign?" I asked him, trying to sound as hopeful as humanly possible.

"No! How is this a good sign? Her backpack in the mud, in some random ass location, with nothing in it to tell me where she went?" His voice cracked a bit, tone slightly more aggressive now. I raised my eyebrows, but he continued on, ignoring my expression. "People don't just get up and leave, Eyvette! Not people with lives, husbands, and friends! People don't just disappear without a trace!" He crossed his arms across his chest, finally making eye contact with me again. The disdain on his face was impossible to hide.

"People disappear all the time," I shot back at him. "You said it *yourself*, that multiple people have vanished from all around here. I'm not trying to be a dick, I'm just pointing out things that seem to be odd about it, that's all."

He let out another laugh and leaned forward.

"You're really a piece of work, aren't you?" His tone was aggressive while his words were a bit biting.

"What's that supposed to mean?" I asked defensively, feeling my forehead wrinkling with attitude. I was sure my face said it all.

"You're questioning me about why someone I love went missing? Does that work for you, Eyvette? While you're out here looking for some... some ghost from your past?" I recoiled back, ready to fire off at him, but he kept going before I had a chance to respond. "You think I don't know what you're doing, don't you? Asking *all* these questions. Do you think I'm an idiot?"

I stared at him, my face morphing from anger to more of a smug expression. I did, actually. I did think he was an idiot right now. A man, out searching for his wife who clearly had been trying to leave him. A man who abused his wife to the point of her wanting to disappear.

"Yeah, I do," I spat angrily before I could stop myself. I hadn't noticed until that moment that I was reaching my hand towards my bag in my tent, pulling the notebook from the front pocket. "How long did you know, hmm?" I shouted from my tent, waving the leatherbound notebook in front of my face. His eyes widened and I immediately realized how dumb I had been. I planned to get information and then leave without him noticing. I'd get myself as far away from him as I could before reporting what was in the notebook. To feel him out before deciding whether or not he could truly be involved in either of their disappearances. The thought of him knowing about their affair had wormed its way into my head from that last page in the journal. It poisoned my brain with more questions and doubts. That was all over now. I had shown my hand without thinking.

He leaned forward but didn't move.

"Where did you get that?" he asked me quietly.

"I found it this morning," I said, unwrapping the leather cord from around the notebook and turning through the pages. "It's pretty interesting, you know, the things you find out reading someone's thoughts," I said, my voice low and steady. The knife in the side pocket of my bag was visible from where I sat, and I told myself that if I needed to, I could toss the journal and make a run for it, knife in hand. I continued to flip through the pages, making my way towards the note that Charlie left. "Let's see," I said, turning the final page of Meredith's thoughts.

His face said it all; he knew. He knew everything and that was clear.

"Stop it," he hissed. "Stop!"

I turned the page and turned the notebook towards him.

"Tell me, when were you going to tell the police that you knew your wife was having an affair?" I was breathing heavily, my nerves almost non-existent. "That there was a connection between Meredith and Charlie?" I stood up, pushing my back against the front of my tent, letting him know that I wasn't afraid of him. Not here, not now.

"I said stop it!" he screamed, standing up, his chest rising and falling quicker in anger. "Charlene Ellis is whore who brainwashed my wife into believing she was something she's not!"

I took one step back, my foot going into the base of my tent, bracing myself before responding. A small smile grew across my face, not because I was happy, no, but because I had gotten him. That was all it took to get him to admit that he knew Charlie.

"Oh, right! Your wife leaving you makes someone else a whore?!" I was shouting, slamming the notebook to my feet as I yelled. "Classic! Another straight man who beats his wife blaming someone else!" I could see his anger growing, but he made no movements, not toward me or the notebook lying on the ground before me. I stood still, my face in a scowl.

"Eyvette, you have no idea what you're talking about," he warned.

"No? You didn't toss her around? Yell at her?" I pointed to the notebook on the ground before, repeating the words that Charlie had written in the last entry. Something in my brain clicked. The image of him throwing the ring back into the bag flashed before me mid-yell. "Whose ring is it?" I asked him in an almost snarl.

He said nothing, his face filled with anger.

"Whose ring is it?!" I was yelling, full-on yelling, my throat burning from the force of it.

"It was hers!" he yelled back at me. "It was that stupid bitch's ring!" His hands were clenched into fists, stuck to the side of his body.

"You knew she was leaving didn't you?" I started.

"Stop it!" he yelled.

"You knew she and Charlie were together!" I screamed back.

"I said stop it!"

"You killed her, didn't you, you sick fuck!" I turned and reached for my bag, barely noticing him lunging forward toward me. I kicked the book as quickly as I could, giving me just a moment to push myself in the opposite direction. With my pack in my right hand, I barely missed his hands reaching towards me, his voice screaming something I couldn't make out. I turned back just for a second to see him falling to the ground next to the notebook. I weaved into the trees to my right and sprinted as fast as I could through the coming darkness while Clinton Bates screamed in my direction.

CHAPTER FOURTEEN

GIRL IN THE PINES

H er face hit the forest floor, her arms unable to break the fall. With the twinge vibrating through her right foot she knew she had tripped over something without even having to look.

The night was black, woods scattered in darkness, the ground cold. Cold and damp from the dew that came in from the fog making its way through the trees. It weaved around like a cloud, engulfing the bottoms of the pines and covering the ground. For just a moment, she lay there, forgetting where she was, her hands slipping under her face like a child taking a nap. The ground was safe and stable. The fog floating just above allowed her to only see across the floor of the pines, the sky completely erased by pillows of swirling condensation. It was the first time she truly felt cold. With her body out of motion, her muscles were too tired to feel the pain that spread throughout them. She lay there, not refusing to stand, but unable to.

Under the cover of clouds and darkness, she rolled herself to the side until she made contact with the base of a large tree. Her hands reached up, nails digging into its bark, as she pulled herself up with her last bit of energy.

Her side hit the trunk first, able to feel the lines in the chunks of bark against her back. Sitting against it, she pulled her knees into her chest, her feet sliding across the jagged sticks and dirt that littered the forest floor.

The fog would only cover her for so long, but she had to close her eyes. She had to rest.

When her eyes finally opened, her view of the forest felt like a dream, no, a sci-fi movie where someone got trapped in a snow globe. The thought comforted her as she breathed in the damp air around her. The long-sleeved denim shirt she was wearing was now soaking wet, drenched with the water of thick, clouded fog. She pulled her arms in, wrapping them around herself, the sound of her teeth chattering finally audible to her ears. Her body felt heavy, tired, and rigid. Fear began to creep into her, formerly lucid, thoughts reminding her she wasn't safe here.

The pain in her shoulder was back with a vengeance, keeping her from falling back asleep against the trunk of the large pine. She reached up towards it, fingers coming back damp from the seeping blood that ran in long lines of stains down the denim. Her fingers moved upward, feeling their way to find the wound. She knew she needed to apply pressure and ultimately slow the bleeding. She recoiled her hand back as it grazed something sharp, face wincing in pain.

She reached back up to examine the sharp object. She used her other hand to pull the collar of the denim shirt to the side, letting the shoulder of the sleeve slip down over her arm. Pushing out just above her skin, sat a perfectly shaped metallic triangle. She sat back against the tree, the pain radiating across her shoulder as her fingers made contact with it. She could feel it, pulling from the inside of her shoulder, wedged under layers of skin and muscle. She clenched her teeth together, the chattering sending waves of cold down her neck. She gripped her fingers around the triangle, wary of the sharp edges, and then, with as much force as she could muster, she pulled.

The triangle gave way with the pressure, dragging the pencil-thin black rod from inside her shoulder. She shakily exhaled as the last inch slipped from the hole in her, teeth still clenched as the air pushed through, blood starting to flow freely down her skin. She threw her hand over her mouth as a pained scream instinctively began.

If he was near, she couldn't risk being heard. She held the black rod in her hand, rolling it between her fingers while examining the metal tip. An arrow, now sleek and glistening in blood, was what hit her as she ran through the Pines. This was the cause of that ache throbbing down her shoulder as she fled from him again.

He would kill her if he found her, exactly like the other girls.

Chapter Fifteen

EYVETTE

The woods seemed to grow around me, darkness spreading through the trees like it was spilling from the sky. I could barely catch my breath, but his screams from behind me pushed me forward. I arrived at the main trail and turned North, following the gradual hill incline.

I reached towards the side of my pack as I ran, one strap wrapped around my neck and shoulder, barely hanging on. I adjusted the pack across both shoulders, pulling the straps down to tighten it across the base of my back. I could feel my flashlight in its side pocket, instinctively reaching for it, but stopping myself before my hand wrapped around it. *No flashlight, not now. That would only give my location away.* Clinton's flashlight was busted. That gave me an advantage here, the night allowing me to hide in plain sight. I pushed myself forward, the screams from behind me finally stopping.

Had he given up the chase?

Would he get himself lost trying to find me?

It didn't matter, so long as I stayed ahead of him. I reached back toward my pack again, using my left hand to search through the small pocket as I ran. I pulled the knife out of my bag and gripped the handle in my right fist, blade pointed toward the ground. I was going to be ready. No matter what.

The trees thinned near the top of the hill, creating a small opening that made a great lookout point, the trees below seeming smaller due to how high you were. I stopped to catch my breath, turning myself in a full circle, deciding which direction would make the most sense.

If I kept North, I would need to stay on the trail for days until I reached the next town. If I went West, then I'd go further into the Pines. Charlie once asked if I was interested in exploring the western portion, but the idea had scared me more than excited me. Hell, I was terrified now. Here I stood in the opening, deciding my fate as it were. The last thing I needed to do was get lost out here. I had information, and I needed to get back down to the base of the trail to tell my story.

All the skeptics had been right: Clinton Bates was a murderer, a husband scorned, seeking revenge. He played the part so well, breaking his stoic demeanor in interviews to let a tear fall when the moment was right. Izzy had called it the moment she saw the missing fliers go up.

"Mhmm, he did it," she declared, pointing at the television with one hand while the other scooped a large amount of popcorn from the bowl in our bed.

I laughed and looked at her, setting my phone on the nightstand.

"You don't know that," I countered.

"Oh yeah, the fuck I do! It's always the husband!" She kept chewing, trying to talk through the crunching of her bedroom snack. "Look at him, all done up looking like a damn Ken doll. Guilty as hell!"

"I dunno, he seems really upset," I responded, watching half-chewed popcorn pieces fall as she laughed. I laughed along with her, content to watch her as she grabbed another handful and shoved it in her mouth.

"Uh yeah. Upset his ass is about to get got! He's going to jail babe, bet."

Thoughts of her flooded my head as I stood there, still turning myself in circles, struggling to choose the safest choice. Clinton would likely find the trail at some point, if not soon, then he would probably continue on North after me. But I went West, it would be days before I reached a town. Going East wouldn't be easy, but more populated towns were nestled into the foothills, much more so than the towns to the North.

Without hesitating longer, I turned and ran into the tall trees that towered over the right side of the hill. With the ground evening out, I found a solid stride as I ran, my hands moving the small branches that blocked the path.

This path was rough, my feet clipping roots and rocks as I ran, throwing my body off balance. My breathing had finally caught up to me, my body relaxing as I pushed East. I would go as far as I could tonight, then stop somewhere dense in the woods when I felt safe enough to rest. The thoughts of Izzy kept coming, her warning playing over and over again in my head.

She was right, usually was, walking back into some "backwoods ass town" wasn't smart, but I had found something.

Look at what I had to tell the world now.

Clinton knew his wife was having an affair, and not just an affair, that she was with another woman. *Charlie, what did you get yourself into out here?* I scolded her mentally. *Seeing a married woman and trampling off into the forest with her while she was still with her husband. What were you thinking?*

It didn't seem like her, but the proof was there: Charlie's handwriting in Meredith's journal and the engagement ring in the little black box inside Meredith's pack. This is exactly what Penelope was expecting from me. I had enough information to make a podcast episode that would break records on the charts.

I smiled as I walked, fear slowly dissipating while a feeling of pride replaced it. The moment faded away just as quickly as it came, Izzy's voice in my head. "Holier than thou," she said before I exited the car.

Was she right?

Had I come here for the right reasons at all?

Did it matter?

If a story could be told, or if the truth could be found, wasn't that enough?

I slowed my run to a walk and started talking it out in my head, trying to piece together everything so it all made sense. I reached towards the side pocket of my pack when I realized something crucial. My voice recorder was in the mesh netting of my tent.

Clinton could have gone back, rummaged through my tent, and found it. If that was true then he had the notebook and the recorder. Along with Meredith's backpack and engagement ring. The only sources of truth that existed were his.

He had all of it.

I stopped walking, standing on the trail with my hands to my head, palms pressing into my ears. I had to go back. I knew the truth, but going home and telling my side without physical proof wouldn't accomplish anything. It wouldn't bring justice for the missing girls. It didn't get Clinton Bates arrested and it sure as hell didn't help uncover the truth of what happened out here.

No, the only thing it did do was line me up for another lawsuit.

Fuck! I was such an idiot.

I shouldn't have shown my hand the way I did. I should have kept hiking with him, not telling him about the journal or asking him any questions. I could have found a reason to turn back towards Travelers Rest and take photos of the notebook before turning it over to the authorities. They would have enough information from the journal entry to question Clinton all over again.

I hadn't thought this through. Instead, I had been reckless.

That settles it...I'm going back.

I turned around and began walking back, turning my attention back to the forest around me. I needed to be silent. I needed to get back to the tent and see what was there. Maybe he only took the journal and hadn't found the voice recorder? That was enough. My recorder was all I needed.

I walked through the opening at the top of the hill again, stopping at the edge of the treeline to make sure no one was near. Still unable to use my flashlight, I squinted my eyes and tried to see in the small trails that bled into the opening.

Nothing. No one was here.

I slipped my pack off of my shoulders, slowly placing it on the ground beside me. I would leave it here, making it easier for me to slip in and out of the campsite without being heard. I pushed it towards the trunk of a large pine, pulled the flashlight from the small pocket of the bag, placed it in my pocket, and then set off across the opening. I held the knife in my hand still, ready to use it if I needed to.

Somehow, it seemed so much darker walking back towards the campsite we made. I stayed inside the tree line of the trail, using the trees to lean against and hide behind as I worked my way to the small opening where my tent lay. Both tents were still pitched, the flap of Clinton's still open to face mine.

I waited for a moment before coming out from behind the trees and ducking behind the back of my tent, crouching down to listen for any sounds of footsteps or breathing. The cicadas were loud here, and I couldn't make out any sound apart from their screaming.

I crawled on my hands and knees to the side of my tent, peeking around the front for just a moment.

The notebook. Simply lying on the ground, its pages open against the dirt. I moved forward, pulling it toward me, closing it, and sliding it into my jacket pocket. I came around the front of the tent and reached my hand inside the mesh liner, feeling around for the recorder.

I found it, still recording, exactly where I left it.

I pressed the large circular record button and slipped it into my pocket with the leatherbound journal. I peered around the other side of my tent then slipped back behind the trees. I had them, both of them. He left them there, probably in a panic to find me.

Thank God! Now I have exactly what I need to nail him!

I went to take a step forward when a flash of light shot through the trees ahead of me, creating a strobe effect as it moved across the forest, glowing between the rows of trees. The crunch of the ground and snapping twigs under heavy feet came closer, as I pressed my entire body up against the back of a tall pine. I clasped my hand to my mouth and pressed myself as hard as I could into the trunk, silently cursing the chipping bark that fell to the forest floor.

The flashlight glow continued to move throughout the treeline, from left to right, like a lighthouse at sea. The trees lit up beside me, the ground only visible where the light beam touched. I tried my hardest not to breathe, the panic in my chest starting to rise, my hand vibrating against the tree with the knife still clutched in it.

Don't move Yvee, I kept repeating to myself. Stay quiet, don't breathe, don't move. I repeated them over and over in my head, taking small shallow breaths as I kept my hand pressed against my mouth.

I heard the vinyl of the tents being tossed about, the rods snapping and breaking. I wasn't sure what was taking over me, but I felt my arm push off against the tree and, before I knew it, I was in a full sprint through the row of trees in front of me, dodging between the small branches that lay around on the ground.

The flashlight circled the forest as I ran, hitting the trees around me with light. I let the branches that blocked my way hit my face as I ran, tasting blood on my lips while I pushed my way through the brush along the ground. The farther I ran, the more distant the flashlight got, slowly fading behind me.

That fucking liar, I thought, remembering Clinton's story of a broken flashlight. I had seen it, covered in mud and cracked, but hadn't thought to check if it actually still worked or not. It did, and he had almost caught me. If he had been there a moment earlier, or I hadn't run back into the treeline, this would be a very different situation. I wonder if he had seen me slip into the trees before turning on his flashlight, or if he managed to see the backside of me as I ran off into the woods.

I stopped for a moment, resting myself up against the tree as I took in as many deep breaths as I could. I don't know how far I had come, but I could no longer see the beams from the flashlight, meaning he probably hadn't seen me take off through the woods. I had to get back to my pack and get the fuck out of the woods.

"Eyvette!" The scream echoed through the woods, shattering the chorus of cicadas that encircled me. "Eyvette!" The cry was coming from a distance, but there was no mistaking, it was him. Clinton Bates knew I had it, all of it.

He knew I had the truth.

Chapter Sixteen

Girl in The Pines

H er feet were cold, like the rest of her, as she slowly limped through the forest. The fog was still heavy, creating a wet cloud around her, drenching her clothes to the point of sticking to her skin again. The darkness had slipped away without her knowledge. The forest floor now glowed a hazy gray as the sun rose. With fog this dense, visibility was only possible a few feet ahead of each step she took.

The forest was quiet this morning, void of all sound. No good morning chirps from the birds that dwelled deep within the Pines, no crickets or cicadas singing. A slight breeze moved through the tops of the trees, swaying them just enough to make the fog swirl around the forest floor.

Her body was heavy. Each step made her feet feel like they were made of lead. Her hands were shaking, sending waves of shivers up her back, making the hairs on her neck stand at attention. Her teeth were still chattering, clicking together, vibrating her jaw and sending pain into her ears. Her shoulder was still hurting, but as she pulled the denim shirt away from her chest, she saw the blood had finally stopped flowing. The blood was finally dry, hardened over the hole the arrow had made in her.

Her thoughts took over as she walked, the forest fading around her again, her mind trying to escape the pain.

Why had she come here? Her, of all the people to come here?

She couldn't help but feel stupid, knowing how awful the idea was. She knew it before the plane touched down only a few mornings earlier. She knew it the moment she stepped foot onto the trail. Her face stung, tears falling without permission, creating clean lines down her dirty face. All she could think about was home. Oh, how she longed to be there.

To be safe and warm in her bedroom. Not here in this nightmare.

She couldn't have saved anyone anyway...let alone herself.

Chapter Seventeen

Eyvette

I pushed off the tree I leaned against and ran, his voice finally silent.

He had screamed my name multiple times in desperate need to find me.

I'm so stupid! I shouldn't have let him into my tent. I shouldn't have trusted him at all!

I knew coming into the woods he didn't sit well with me, but I allowed myself into this situation. The tears streaming down my face were a mixture of fear and pride.

I was terrified. I couldn't lie to myself to make it better. I wouldn't do that. I wouldn't try to talk myself out of the fear. I needed it. I wasn't safe here, not out here in the woods alone with a murderer. The pride came and went in waves. It reminded me that even though I was an idiot, I still got the information needed. I was on the move. I wouldn't let him catch me. I would make it to the nearest town in the East and get the next flight home.

I thought about Charlie. The last thing she may have ever written was in my jacket: a goodbye to Meredith Bates. Meredith Bates: the first missing, married woman involved in an affair. I wondered if she knew her husband was onto her or if she cared. I thought about Charlie: alone in the woods, leaving Meredith and walking back to town, only to get stopped by Clinton Bates.

The images swirled through my mind like a movie: the moment they met on the trail, both of them knowing who the other was without wanting to show they did. In a game of cat and mouse, Charlie gets attacked on the forest floor by Clinton, fueled by rage and desire to take back what belonged to him. She would have run or put up a fight until she couldn't.

I thought back to Meredith, still sleeping, surrounded by her friends for the weekend. They hadn't been receptive to Charlie, probably shocked by her affair, or confused by her marriage. After all, they never came forward with information after her disappearance, nor after Charlie.

I ran further, pushing thicker branches to the side while I broke the smaller limbs hanging in front of me. My mind raced faster than I could comprehend, images and thoughts hitting me like bricks as I ran.

Had Charlie made it out of the woods?

Had she maybe, somehow, dodged Clinton Bates on her way back to town?

Maybe he found Meredith, who wandered into the forest after realizing Charlie left. He could have gotten her away from her friends, just far enough so they couldn't hear him taking her life.

The police report said that Meredith went missing from her tent overnight. It made sense to me, knowing what Charlie wrote in the last entry of the journal. Meredith would have woken up at some point, realized Charlie was missing, and either blamed herself or her friends for Charlie's sudden departure. She would have gone after her, right?

I thought about it more, wondering what I would have done if I were in this situation.

Would I have gone after her or let her go?

How did nobody notice Charlie was missing until weeks later? Her parents said nothing about not hearing from her. *That's odd*, I thought, *why say nothing when Meredith vanished if she made it out of the woods?*

The reasons I came up with were endless. My mind sorted through as many as it could, but they always ended the same way: two smiling faces on missing posters and Clinton Bates pretending to search for his long-lost wife.

The forest was darker, the trees looming over me while the night grew colder. I was exhausted, but if I let myself start thinking about home and Izzy, I would slip into blind fear and start to question every decision I made. I was exhausted, but if I let myself think about home and Izzy, I would slip into blind fear and question every decision leading up to now. I kept moving through the forest, heading to the East, hopeful to hit a town soon. I kept my knife clutched tight against my palm as I reached the opening where I had left my pack, stopping inside the treeline and squinting, watching the forest around me to see if there was any movement. I circled around the trees and checked the ground.

It wasn't there.

I specifically placed my pack on the ground near the tall pine, but now it was gone.

"Fuck," I said in a whisper. "Fuck, fuck, fuck!"

It was gone. I knew I left it here, right by the thick pine tree I currently leaned against in frustration. All of my shit, every single thing I needed to survive out here.

Gone.

I had my knife, the recorder, and Meredith's journal, but absolutely nothing else. My food, water, and clothes were missing alongside my bag. Someone had taken everything when I went back to the tent for the recorder.

I cursed myself again, putting my hands over my face in disbelief. I was going to have to walk all night until I found someplace safe. *If that even exists.* The thought of sleeping on the ground, out in the wilderness surrounded by darkness, scared me.

I wouldn't be able to stop, not tonight. I had to get closer to the next town.

The trails around me started to disintegrate, washed away by rain running downhill, and people taking better-made paths. Tonight was going to be a long night for me.

I needed to stay calm.

I needed to focus.

Clinton Bates was still out in the Pines. No matter how near or far he was, I knew one thing. He was dangerous. As far as I knew, I was the only source of the truth. There was nothing, and nobody, to stop him now from silencing me.

I needed to get out.

The trail narrowed, and I could feel branches pulling at my jacket as I pushed through them. I wondered if the last person who trekked in this direction had taken this trail or if they had tried to walk in the dark out here in the Pines. The crickets and cicadas sang loudly around me, the cool air blowing through the tops of the trees, the sound of falling pine needles barely audible.

This was the first time in the woods that I truly felt alone. Not in that peaceful way you felt waking up in the morning, unzipping your tent, and feeling the cool air while birds sang. No, this feeling was cold. It traveled through my body and made my stomach tense and flip when I thought about it for too long. Here I was, heading in a direction I had never been before, searching for a town I knew existed yet had never been to. I had no tent for shelter either, so if another storm came then I was fucked. My phone, which probably didn't have service anyway, was still sitting in the bottom of my pack–wherever that was.

A tingle ran up my spine at the thought of someone having my phone. All my personal information, my clothing, my food. I tried to shake it off as I walked, the rocks beneath me shifting beneath the weight of my feet. I was going downhill, the Earth slowly leaning me forward, my steps getting heavier as I tried to balance myself. I reminded myself to breathe and reached my hands out, using nearby tree branches to help guide me along the path. I could barely see the ground in front of me, and if I fell–well, I didn't want to think what I would hit along the way.

Izzy's laugh filled my head. I could almost picture her lips, spread from ear to ear with her teeth barely visible. She would be losing it right now, watching me slip on these rocks, giggling every time I almost fell. She was the best thing I had in my life, but now I wasn't sure what that would look like when I got home. The last thing we said to each other hadn't come from kindness, but I knew she loved me. She was worried, and here now, in the woods, I understood why.

I came here in search of answers, already unsafe since multiple girls have gone missing. Yet I still chose to leave the comfort of our life to search for someone I barely knew anymore. I knew that decision came with conse-quences, but all I could think about was my career being pulled away. As her stardom rose, mine settled into a rhythm, not gaining further traction. She was booking roles, and taking on contracts for makeup, clothing, and skincare. All while I was hosting a podcast.

"Stop making comparisons, we do very different things," she would tell me after I mentioned I didn't do enough. "This isn't a competition."

"Well, if it was, I'd be losing," I had responded.

"Why does everything have to be about work? Jesus Christ, Yvee, could we not have a single day together without you making me feel like shit?"

I was standing in the kitchen, making myself a cup of coffee as she moved away from the table. Her silk pajama shirt was starting to slip off her shoulder and happened to be one of my favorite things about morning coffee time. I wasn't trying to start an argument, but it was all I could think about at that moment. I felt stupid for bringing up the discrepancies in the amount of money I contributed to our apartment, but after I stumbled across the latest electric bill, I couldn't control myself.

"Why didn't you tell me the bills are more expensive than the last place?" I pressed as I poured water into the French press.

"I didn't think it was a big deal," Izzy said, taking a sip of her herbal tea and scrolling through her phone.

"Well, it is. I want to pull my weight here, and I feel like you just take it upon yourself to pay for things I can't afford."

"Yvee, I promise it isn't even like that. We needed a bigger space, and everything is so fucking expensive here. Penelope landed me the new deal with that stupid skincare line, so it basically pays for itself."

She didn't get it, and I was starting to think she never would. Money was easy for her because when you had it, you didn't worry about it.

"Okay, but that's *exactly* my point, *I* couldn't have afforded it. I told you before, I don't want us to get into a situation where if something happens, I can't even bail myself out of a bad situation." In an instant, I knew I had either said the wrong thing or worded it incorrectly without thinking.

Her face dropped and she dropped her phone down to the tabletop.

"Seriously?" She pulled her shirt back over her shoulder and scowled at me. "Why is everything about if something goes wrong, or if we break up, or sounding like you're stuck in some awful situation? Why can't we ever just have breakfast like normal fucking people?" She was angry, or rapidly approaching being angry. I tried to respond, but she hadn't finished what she was trying to get out. "You aren't stuck, Yvee, the door is right there. I don't understand why you get so defensive. I make more money, who cares? Everything in this apartment is ours, not mine. You get that, right?" She stopped talking and crossed her arms, waiting for my response, knowing that I was probably bouncing through over a thousand ways to respond without upsetting her further.

"Yes, I get it. I didn't mean it like that. I just feel like I could be doing more. Or that I should be doing more, I guess." I truly felt that way. I always had.

"Okay, so do something different. You love the podcast, and it's doing so well! People ask me about it all the time in my interviews. You know that. So, what else do you want to do?" She was right, it was going well. It had been for months. The money was good, it just paled in comparison to what someone climbing the ladder of success in the film industry could pull in.

"I don't know, maybe I'll be an actor," I said, putting the back of my hand to my forehead and beginning to pretend to faint. She laughed.

"Well, fuck knows you're dramatic enough," she said back. She was always so quick with the comebacks. She stood up and walked across the room, running her hand along the marble counter of the bar in the kitchen.

I made a face at her and shook my head, turning back to the French press.

"Just lighten up, okay? I love you. Money is the last thing we should be thinking about. Do you think I'd be half as good at what I do if I didn't have you to come home to every day and love?" She kissed the side of my face and twirled off back towards the table.

She was perfect, to me at least. And she was also right, as usual. We were good. Everything was good.

At least it was until I decided listening to Penelope and trekking into the woods after someone who was no longer part of my life was a smart idea. I would need to work really hard for Izzy's forgiveness, but it would all be worth it.

I thought about Charlie, and how I could give her parents actual answers. It hurt me to think about having a conversation with her parents, letting them know that she was seeing a married woman when she went missing. That her husband knew and had tracked them down.

My stomach felt as if it were filled with stones, and before I could stop myself, my hands were clawing for the ground that had fallen out below me. My knees hit first, the rocks cutting into me with ease while the rest of my body followed suit. I wasn't sure what I hit, but whatever it was had thrown my entire body down the hill I was on. I slid a few feet before my hands made contact with the ground. I was on my hands and knees when I finally stopped, feeling my way around the forest floor for anything to help me stand up. My limbs shook as I finally gained my footing to stand. With a deep breath, I lifted my head just in time to see a light, no, a flashlight, coming right toward my face.

It made contact, pain shooting out from the bridge of my nose across my eyes and ears. I didn't have time to react, his hands wrapping around my body and pulling me into him. The cicadas screamed louder as the flash-light retreated and then returned, this time with more force. I didn't feel my body as it hit the ground, and I only realized I was on my back when a figure stood over me.

Everything blurred, and my assailant's heavy breathing faded as the flashlight hit me for the third time.

The forest went black around me.

Chapter Eighteen

Girl in The Pines

S he walked, even though her body told her not to. The fog had lifted its way toward the tops of the treeline, and the forest glowed under gray clouds. The ground was still damp, and with every step, she could feel the edges of sharp rocks cutting into her. She didn't know how far she had come or if she was going in the right direction–if that even existed out here. She didn't know what day it was, even after trying to backtrack in her mind. Everything was blurring together in the forest.

The screams echoed in her mind, the cuts on her body, all in various timelines of healing. She had come here for answers, for the truth, and she had nothing to show for it. They were dead, and if they weren't, they would be soon. She knew that, and no matter what she tried to tell herself, it was all she could think about. She left them there, in the middle of nowhere, hurt and terrified.

The tears stung her face as she limped her way across the path of pines. The screams resounded in her, like a song that gets stuck in your head after hearing it. She wondered if it would ever stop. If the sounds of her would ever leave her. Her thoughts raced, from staying and fighting the man in the black mask to wondering if she would have been tied up with chains if she had been caught.

He would have killed her, just another girl lost in the woods that no one would ever see again.

She couldn't feel the cold any longer, her body was finally numb to the forest around her. Her thoughts came at her quickly, like a nightmare that she couldn't shake off.

She was back in that awful wood shack, her hands covered in someone else's blood.

She hadn't planned on getting lost in the woods when she first showed up here. She came in through the trailhead only a few mornings ago, the cold drizzle moving in with gray clouds. After being told repeatedly that walking into the woods alone wasn't safe, and knowing that herself, she entered in hopes of finding the truth.

No one disappears without a trace, it wasn't possible.

She walked into the trail, her boots already starting to eat away at the back of her ankle, the friction burning a hole in her socks. The sky looked like it could open up at any minute, but she wasn't going to wait any longer to get started. No one was doing anything that she saw as helpful, and if no one would listen to her, she would figure it out herself. The trail was darker than she imagined it would be, having only ever heard about it.

She wasn't a hiker, nor was she interested in camping in the forest, no matter where it was. The boots continued to dig into her ankles, and she would stop every now and again to adjust her socks, praying that they would create enough space between the back of the shoe and her skin to stop the burning.

She never imagined that entering this place would lead her to where she was now, her body shivering but still unable to feel the coldness around her.

She stopped for a moment, letting her thoughts carry her away, but they carried her to darker moments that she was trying to avoid.

The small wooden building in the middle of the woods that she found while trying to outrun the rain, unable to pitch her tent while the water poured down around her. It was near impossible to see anything in front of her as she ran, closely avoiding the edge of what seemed to be a drop-off into nothing. She had barely caught her breath, choking down the rain that was coming at her in all directions, when she could make out the faint shape of the cabin before her.

The smell of smoke was so strong that she could almost taste it in her mouth. When her hands made contact with the first wall, she guided herself alongside the building until she reached a banister coming off of a small porch. She stepped up onto the loose boards covering the floor and found her footing and balance before letting go of the railing. She took a minute, shaking all of the water off of her, pulling her hair back, and twisting the water loose. She wiped her face and looked across the small wrapped porch.

This place was dilapidated, the wood rotting all around the sides, the glass window in the front broken into large shards of glass that barely hung to a black tarp-like material that sat behind it. The smell of smoke was stronger here, and it turned her stomach, but it was better than the drowning feeling that running through the storm brought her. She reached for the doorway, pushing in on the handleless wood frame, but nothing moved. It was sealed shut, nails going in all directions through the wood beams that lined the entryway. She kicked at the bottom of the door, but it was solid and firm, with no movement at all.

As she moved toward the window, she noticed a small black hole in the bottom corner of the black tarp. She knelt down to meet it at eye level and pressed her hands over her eyes as she peered through the broken glass. She couldn't make out anything specific, but there was light coming from the far corner of the room. She couldn't tell if it was fire, which would explain the smoke, or if it was some sort of lantern that was left burning. Whatever it was, it meant that someone had been there and still could be.

Before she had time to consider the consequences, she reached her hand behind the shards of glass and began ripping away at the small hole, the fibers in it so dry rotted that they fell like ash on the ground. She pulled her denim overshirt off and wrapped it around her hand, creating a glove that allowed her to punch into the bottom of the window, shattering the rest of the already broken glass. She pulled her hand back and bent over to look inside again, this time seeing the entirety of the room.

It was almost empty, apart from a small bed frame that sat in the corner. It looked as if it had been there for centuries, the cloth ripped and showing exposed springs from the mattress. The sight of it made her stomach churn. There was a doorway not far behind it that had been the source of light, its cracks, and spaces glowing with a warm yellow color.

She reached her hand into the window, feeling her way up until she felt the clasp that held the window shut. When she tried to push it up with both of her hands, the window gave a cracking sound, and old paint chips fell to the floor like dust. The window finally moved, slowly at first, then quickly until it hit the top pane. The window was just high enough that she needed to lift her leg and fold her body forward to make the transition from the porch into the room. As creepy as it felt to her it was, at the very least, warm and dry.

Before she had a moment to look around the room, a scream erupted from the glowing doorway. Scared and caught completely off guard, she threw her body back toward the wall, her hands barely catching the edge of the window, glass cutting into her palms.

The scream lasted for only a moment before it was muffled by music that radiated from beyond the door. It was loud, even with the wall separating her from it, the vibrations rattled the floor and the broken glass beside her. She covered her ears and slid down the wall until she was sitting on the floor. Her initial reaction was to run, but if someone was here and heard her come in through the window, then maybe hiding here was the best option.

Too many thoughts flooded her mind as the music blared through the cabin. She crawled her way from the corner toward the small bed, slipping herself beneath it, moving her hips back and forth as she pushed herself all the way to the wall. She covered her ears and closed her eyes, begging herself to not scream. She didn't know what was happening, but that scream couldn't be anything good. She wasn't alone here, and she regretted having broken in.

As quickly as the scream had been muffled by the heavy music, it disappeared, the cabin going completely silent. She stayed where she was, still unable to move, waiting for any sound at all to stir her. Her body had almost stopped trembling when she heard the footsteps just outside the lit doorway.

They were heavy, shaking the floorboards beneath her to the point that she could feel them rattling against her exposed lower back as she lay there. The moment the footsteps disappeared out of the room, the music began to blare again, the same song repeating. She lay perfectly still, her hands still covering her ears as the song stopped for a moment, then repeated. It felt like hours as she lay there, her body vibrating against the floorboards. She couldn't make out any of the words that were being screamed in the song, but the beat was the same, over and over again, 1-2-3-4, 1-2-3-4, boom boom boom.

She shook the memory away from her as hard as she could, her arms still wrapped around herself as she walked through the forest. There was a strange calmness that had started to wash over her, her body tired from the constant fear and running. She didn't know how much longer she could do this, and she contemplated if it was even worth it to keep trying. She was so cold, her body at the point where the pins and needles that covered her had disappeared and were now replaced with numbness.

The fog had gone, and she didn't know what time it was, or in what direction she was going. She thought about home, about the life she had dreamed of being ripped away from her. She would have cried if she could, but there were no tears left in her. She was too exhausted to show any kind of emotion. There was no voice in her head that pleaded with her to keep going, no fight left in her body telling her to run.

She walked because it was the only thing she could do.

She didn't care if he caught up to her.

She didn't care because she was already dead.

But for now, she tried.

Walking was, at the very least, trying. Trying was enough for now.

She survived being alone for days, survived the cabin, and survived his knife. For now, she would walk until she physically couldn't anymore.

Chapter Nineteen

Eyvette

The pain from the bridge of my nose was the first thing I felt as I tried to open my eyes, bringing my hands to my face to feel it, my eyes blurry and unable to focus on anything.

Blood. My hands were coated in it, warm and thick, still coming from what felt like a split in my skin, between my eyes. I tried to lift my head, but everything felt so heavy right now. I tried to focus my eyes on what was above me, but I couldn't make out any details with how blurry my vision was. Everything looked like wood, and my body was laying on something hard. I blinked, remembering the beam of light coming toward my face before it made contact.

"Fuck," I said aloud in pain, my head ached and the pain between my eyes was making it hard for me to keep them open. I tried to place my hands beside me and push myself up, but I could only make it onto my side. I lay there for a minute, noticing the pool of blood that had started to collect beneath my cheek on the wood floor. Before I could think, I started shouting from the floor.

"Clinton!" I screamed his name multiple times, as loud as my body would let me. "Clinton Bates, you fucking coward!" I could feel the burn of tears coming down my face, mixing with the open wounds, setting fire to my skin. "Where are you, you piece of shit!"

My thoughts raced, and I wondered if he would finish the job quickly, or if he would take his time. If I was going to die, I wasn't going to die without a fight. I would die only after making him feel as small as he was.

I wasn't normally a fighter, not like this, but I refused to go out afraid.

I don't know what took over in my head that made me feel like continuing to scream his name. I wouldn't give him the satisfaction of knowing how scared I was. I managed to lift my body and press it to the wall beside me. Everything hurt, but mostly my eyes, still swollen from getting hit in the face. My vision wouldn't settle. Every direction I turned seemed to swirl in a nauseating display until my sight settled on something specific. Slowly, I started to piece together the room around me.

It was small, wrapped in wood paneling that was filled with cracks and gaps that let in soft yellow light. The floor beneath me was hard and cold, and when I placed my hand on it, I could feel the splinters of cracked wood pieces. The room was no bigger than a closet, with a single bulb hanging above me from what looked like a black extension cord wrapped around a large nail. The walls around me were coated in splashes of maroon-colored shapes, some darker than others. I reached for the wall next to me and traced the pattern that colored the rotting boards.

The blood from my nose had made its way to my hand and seeped into the dry wood, turning from fresh red blood to a deep crimson color. As I stared at it, it started to spread slowly, its color changing again to match the maroon patterns on the wall.

Blood...

It was all blood...

The streaks on the floor...the shapes on the wall...

My stomach churned and I tried my hardest not to vomit. I was breathing heavily and could feel terror taking over my body again despite my efforts to calm down. My screams had finally stopped, and I found myself crawling around the floor looking for any sign of a doorway in or out of the box I was trapped in.

Was this what it felt like to be an animal stuck in a cage?

Was this the same fate that Meredith and Charlie had succumbed to?

Was it their blood that painted the walls in this closet?

My breathing was interrupted by short blasts of air and the bellowing of small cries that had started to rise out of my chest. The tears coming down my face were starting to burn the skin on my cheeks, and I tried to remind myself that Clinton Bates would take pleasure from seeing this. He was nearby, for sure. There was no way he would just leave me here in this place. I was the loose end he needed to tie off. I searched the cracks in the floor and walls, the light coming through blocking me from seeing beyond the enclosed box I was in. I sat back against the wall and the screams started again.

"What are you waiting for!" I screamed as loud as I could. "Fucking kill me if you're going to, you sick piece of shit! Huh?! Nothing to say now, you coward?!" The echoes of my screaming surrounded me, my head pounding from the pain in my face.

I could feel myself starting to lose consciousness, and I blinked as hard as I could to stay in reality. I screamed one last time, the only thing that came to my mind.

"Murderer!"

The light inside the small room turned off, taking with it the glow of yellow that came from between the cracks in the wood. I sank back into the corner of the room, letting the darkness surround me, as music began to blast throughout the house. The ground and walls rattled all around me, as I slapped my hands to cover my ears. I pressed as hard as I could against my head, but the sound was so loud that it made the hairs on my body vibrate. I pulled my knees into my chest and bent my face forward into them, covering my ears with my arms as I rocked back and forth in the dark.

I was going to die here, I knew it.

CHAPTER TWENTY

GIRL IN THE PINES

V isions of the cabin flashed in her head, her body filled with fatigue and ready to collapse. She wasn't sure what was keeping her in motion at this point. Her body was tired, the cuts, scraps, and gashes that covered her now numb with the cold of the pines around her. The trees around her now all blended together, their colors and shapes a complete blur. She didn't know what direction she was walking in, or if she was walking at all. Her body was in motion, but her mind was wandering in and out of her memories.

The screaming, the music, the cold wood floor beneath her.

She had barely made it out of the room alive.

For what seemed like hours she lay under the bed with her ears covered, thoughts racing, the beat so loud it rattled her body to the point of feeling numb. It wasn't until the music finally stopped and a door slammed that she felt comfortable enough to place her hands down by her side and slip herself from under the bed.

Her body continued to vibrate as she tiptoed toward the door that was once lit with warm yellow light. She pressed her ear to the door and listened. The sound of her own deep breaths rattled her to the point of hearing nothing from beyond the rotting wood. She stood there, still pressed against the door, too afraid to make another move.

What if they were still there?

What if she wasn't alone?

As she stood still, she could faintly make out the sound of the rain against the roof above her. It was pouring outside still, the storm having yet to pass over. She shouldn't have come in here, but with no tent and no sense of what direction she was going, she didn't feel like there was much of a choice. The smell of the smoke from outside barely existed inside, replaced with the now with something foul. She hadn't noticed it when she first entered, but it was strong now, her stomach churning as she swallowed hard and finally stepped back from the doorway.

"Hello," she said softly, praying that no one would respond to her. Her hands vibrated beside her, her fingertips barely peeking out of the soaked denim sleeves that ran down the lengths of her arm. Her voice was barely above a whisper. "Hello, is somebody there?" The eerie silence that came from beyond the door sent waves of nausea through her body. Something was wrong here.

"Please, is anyone there?"

She almost screamed as a faint voice whispered through the rotting boards to the left of her. She stepped backward, pulling her arms up as if preparing for a fist-fight.

"Please help me," the girl whispered. "Please don't leave me here. Please. Please help me." The voice was weak, barely audible through the wall. A raspy whisper, shaky and desperate. "You... You... You can't leave me here. Please."

She stepped toward the wall, the vibrations in her hand starting to send a trembling throughout her whole body. Her breathing was getting heavier, and tears were forming in her eyes as she took another step in the direction of the girl's voice.

"Who are you? What is this place? Hello?" Her body leaned in the direction of the wall, trying to peer through the small cracks in the wood as she spoke toward her. "Hello?" She moved her right eye along the crack of the wood, squinting to see beyond the wall. She almost fell back, catching herself on the floorboards behind her as the girl beyond the wall's eye came into focus.

Green. Beautiful green, like the color of the forest just outside. She gasped aloud while she fell back, steadying herself as she made her way back toward the wall. The girl was still pressed against the other side of the wood panel, her eye glued to the hole in the wall.

"Please, you have to get me out of here," she kept saying, her voice panicked. "He's going to come back. You have to get me out of here before he comes back!"

"Who? Who's coming back?" she asked her. "What is this place?"

"He's going to kill us all!" the girl from the other side of the wall screamed. She let out a moan that grew into a cry before she began to scream something she couldn't make out.

"Shh," she said, trying to comfort her. "Shh, please be quiet. How do I get to you? Is there a way for me to get you out of there?" She was terrified that the girl's screams would be enough to draw whoever he was back into this place. The girl's cries slowed, as she swallowed and gasped for air, trying to calm herself.

"The door," the girl said. "There's a door." Her eye darted to the left. The doorway she had just leaned against to listen through only minutes before. She stood up and leaned over to look toward the door. "Please, don't leave me here."

"I'm not going to leave you, okay?" She stepped slowly toward the doorway, her hands sliding along the wood until she felt the outline of a small handle on the right side of the door. Her hands were shaking as she pushed against it. Nothing moved. She pushed forward on it, and with a slight squeak, the door began to move outward into the next room. The light that had once sent a glow through the door was gone, and the room was almost completely black. The only source of light was coming from the room she was exiting. She stepped through the threshold and peered around the left side of the doorway.

"Hello, are you there?"

"Please, I'm over here. Please help me," the girl's voice whispered from the dark. She pushed the door as far as she could until it made contact with the wood wall behind it. She had just enough light to see another door come into focus. This door was different, with an actual knob and what looked like bungee cords roped across it. Her hands still shook as she made her way toward the voice of the girl, reaching out for the knob on the door. She pulled it, but nothing moved.

"Please," the girl begged, "get me out of here."

"I'm trying," she said, tears starting to flow down her face. She had never been this terrified in her life. It felt like a horror movie, something that couldn't possibly be happening in real life. Not like this, in this place.

A sound came from behind her, further into a corner she could barely see in. A breath. A gasp. She turned her back toward the door and slid her body to the ground, preparing herself for someone to rush in her direction, but the sound continued. Another gasp, and the sound of metal clinking across the floor. The scrape of the metal against the wood made a sound that reminded her of windchimes, but deeper.

She sat as still as she could, cupping her hand over her mouth so as to not make a sound. As she placed her hands behind her toward the floor, her fingers felt something cold. Like rubber, but more solid. She ran her hand alongside it to see if she could use it to open the door. The moment her hand made contact with the cold rubber on the floor she realized immediately the shape. It clicked in her mind before she could stop her hand from continuing up the cold surface.

A hand, connected to an arm.

A scream erupted from her before she had the thought to stop it, her body falling completely backward toward the wall. Through the darkness, she could barely make out who it was, but the hands were large, and the body was large, leaned over and pressed against the wall, stiff and cold. She scooted herself back towards the door the girl sat behind, her legs kicking at the body, willing it away from her. Her scream had stopped and had been replaced with deep breaths and more tears coming down her face. He was dead, whoever he was. Another groan came from the far corner of the room, and she had almost forgotten the breath she heard just moments before.

"Hello?" she said, her voice shaking, barely audible.

"You can't help her," the girl's voice came from behind her.

"Wh... What?" She whispered back to her.

"You can't help her. She's not going to make it. Please, please just get me out of here." She looked back toward the dark corner, wondering who the breath was coming from, or if she could do something to help her. Before she could process her thoughts, the heavy sounds of footsteps echoed outside from behind her, each step rattling the floorboards around her.

"No! No! No!" The girl's voice began to scream over and over again behind her. Angry, but turning into cries as she grew louder. "No! No! Please!"

She crawled on her hands and knees across the floor to what looked like a small table, or a cot that had fallen inward on itself. She barely had time to roll herself to the backside of it before a low light started to make its way across the floor, the footsteps inside and heavy.

The girl screamed from beyond the door as the man stepped through the room, only his boots visible from under her hiding spot. She had left the door open and hoped that he hadn't noticed. She thought for a moment that he hadn't until she heard the glass from inside the window cracking underneath his footsteps.

His steps quickened, the heavy boots beating across the wood floor as he wandered the shack. He went from wall to wall, turning and pacing about the room. He walked toward the door and the girl's voice echoed from behind as loud beating sounds began to echo across the room. It sounded to her as if he was slamming his fists into the door, the girl's screams growing louder. The door swung open and from her spot under the broken bed, she watched the feet step into the room and slam the door behind him.

Before she could think, she had rolled herself out from under the bed and was crawling toward the doorway he had entered from. The light in the room glowed just enough for her to see what had been making the gasping sounds in the corner of the room.

A person, someone, hanging from heavy metal chains that tied themselves around them and dangled to the ground. They hung upside down, the chains that dangled scraping against the floor as they slowly rotated above the floor. She stopped crawling, frozen in time as she stared at the shadow of the body hanging in the corner.

The moment began to blur as she walked through the forest, the girl telling her to run, to get out, begging her to leave her there in chains. She had just made it out of the door and off the dilapidated porch when the man stood in the doorway where the screaming girl was inside.

The woods around her now started to spin and she could feel her body starting to fight back against her. Her vision was blurry, her balance was off, and the wave of guilt the memories brought back with them sent her body plummeting toward the ground. She blinked, the forest going sideways as she tried to focus her eyes on something. She could barely keep her eyes open as the forest turned dark around her.

She couldn't move, not now.

The girl screaming in the doorway behind the man was covered in blood. She screamed for her to help, reaching her hands outward toward the door.

Chapter Twenty-One

Eyvette

I opened my eyes, the room around me still surrounded by darkness. I didn't know how long I had been asleep, nor did I remember actually falling asleep. The music that rang throughout the house was impossible to escape. I could feel it vibrate across my skin, my hair rattling as the beat shook the floor and walls around me. The room was freezing cold, and I could feel my teeth chattering as I tried to sit up.

My body was weak, my stomach empty and churning at the air that filled the small closet. The smell of something burning filled my nose. It was putrid, like rotting meat and burning wood mixing together. I tried to take a deep breath, my head still pounding from the crack that ran its way down the center of my forehead, along the bridge of my nose, and stopping at the top of my upper lip. The blood had dried into a hard and raised scab that now felt like leather as I touched it.

The music had stopped, and the silence around me made it seem like I was the only person for miles. No birds, no leaves falling, no footsteps. Just the sound of my breathing, the deep breaths going in, the rattle of my teeth chopping the air as it left my mouth. My throat was raw, tight from my screaming. I could feel the wood paneling behind my back, my hands flat on the floor on either side of me. I lifted my right hand and tried to run it through my hair, pushing it back, tangled and impossible to sift through at the moment. I twisted it as tightly as I could while I focused on my breathing, trying to retrace all of my steps.

Clinton couldn't keep me in here forever, that much I knew for certain. He knew I knew his secret, that I knew his wife was going to leave him for another woman. He had played the perfect husband so well, the perfect victim of circumstance. While some people saw right through him, I had started to believe his sincerity. He was a con artist and a good one at that. He had come back to these trails multiple times, claiming he was still searching for Meredith, who I was sure was dead. He knew about her and Charlie meeting out here to go camping, about all of their rendezvous. I wondered how long ago it had started, and if Charlie knew how dangerous the game she was playing was.

I had come out here for answers, and I had gotten them.

I knew why she was missing now.

My breathing started to slow, as I imagined Charlie in the same room I was in, the blood trailing across the walls like a chaotic painting. Was it hers? Had he brought her here, deep within the woods where no one would hear him question her? Did he give her a chance to explain what was happening, or did he kill her just as quickly as he took her?

The Charlie I knew would have put up a fight, she would have tried her damndest to escape. But the weeks had gone by since her disappearance, and there was no way she was just out there hiding from him. She wouldn't do that. She would have gone straight to the police.

My thoughts went back to the days of hiking with her in the woods, our weekend getaways to be free from the eyes of a watchful town. She was well-liked in town, always the talk of people we ran into. She was smart, funny, and beautiful, and it let her escape the torture that I endured with the locals. She would have been able to escape the woods, tell her story, and be believed immediately. Protected instantly.

I sat quietly, shivering, in the small wooden box of a room I was in. After calling out for over an hour, my voice finally started to give out. I couldn't scream any longer. No one could hear me, that was obvious at this point. I didn't know how far he had taken me into the forest, or if I was even in the forest still.

My brain fired off small memories of home, of Izzy, and how worried she would be about me. She would be pacing the floor frantically, unable to keep her composure. She would eventually call Penelope, probably threatening her that if anything were to happen to me out here, she'd have to answer her. She was already upset that Penelope had pushed me into this so hard, and I could imagine the guilt she would lay on her if I never made it home. I wondered if she would be okay without me and if she would continue on to become the A-list actress she was blossoming into. If she would forget me completely, swept up by Hollywood and all its fancy lights. I went down a rabbit hole of wondering, filling myself up with more anxiety than my body could take. Anything that would get my mind off of where I was, and what was probably going to happen to me. I stood up, pressing my shoulders against the wall and screaming one last time as loud as I could toward the ceiling.

"Fuck!" My throat opened just enough that the word erupted out of me in anger, echoing around the small room and rattling the wall that I began to throw my fists against.

"Hello?" A small voice from beyond the wall whispered out.

I froze immediately, stepping back into the wall behind me again. I closed my eyes, waiting for the room to swallow me whole. I was losing it.

"Hello, is someone there?" The voice was louder this time, but still weak.

I remained silent, still unsure if the voice was real, or just my imagination finally starting to get the best of me.

"Please, if someone is there, say something."

"Who are you?" I asked, tears welling up in my eyes as I sat back against the wall, my body sliding down into a seated position. I cried into my hands, waiting for the voice to disappear and leave me here in the darkness.

"Please, there isn't time. Are you able to get out of there?" Her voice was soft. She sounded so tired, completely unemotional as she spoke. "Can you?"

I barely had time to focus on her question before I realized that she was real. She was here, in this place with me. I sat up and wiped the tears from my face.

"I can't! I can't get out, there's no door!" My voice began to grow, pushing past the rawness in my throat as I placed my ear to the wood wall before me. "Where are we?"

"I don't know," she responded quickly. "Do you know what day it is? Where were you taken from? Do you remember where you were?" Her questions were coming at me too fast, and I couldn't focus enough on each one to answer them appropriately.

"I... I'm not sure what day it is." I pulled my ear from the wall and thought for a moment. "Taken," I said. "I was taken from the woods. I was in the woods!" I was almost proud of myself for being able to remember while the shooting pain spread across my face again.

"Where at?" Her voice changed from unemotional to angry. Almost as if she didn't believe me. "Where were you?"

"I was hiking West on a small trailhead. I was coming from Travelers Rest when he found me," I told her. My heart was racing in my chest, and I could feel the blood circulating throughout my body, my heartbeat pounding from inside my neck.

"He took you from the woods? I think I was close to the North Carolina Border when he grabbed me," she said. "I don't remember anything else. I woke up here with the others." Her words sank into my stomach.

"Others," I said, thinking aloud.

"Yes, there is someone else here," she responded. "I haven't seen anyone, I've only heard screams." Her voice began to crack as she spoke. "Were you alone? Will someone be looking for you?" She started to cry. Not loud, but I could hear her sniffles as she waited for me to answer.

I was afraid to, unsure if my answer would help at all. I decided that being honest was probably the best. If we were out here alone, we didn't have anyone else to depend on.

"I was alone," I told her.

She sniffled again, trying to stop herself from crying harder.

"I was looking for someone out here. I was heading West away from the trail to find the next town when he hit me." I felt the long line of dried blood that stretched down my nose. "He hit me with a flashlight, I think. That's the last thing I remember." I pulled my knees up to my chest and wrapped my arms around them. "Has he spoken to you?"

"No, he hasn't said anything at all. The music... The music is so loud. I heard a scream, maybe two of them. Maybe. Maybe from two different people, I don't know." Her cries had slowed. "He... He cut my side pretty bad before he threw me in here. I've been in and out of it for a few days, I think. I can't tell anymore."

I covered my mouth to stop the cry from coming out. The tears were streaming down my face, and I couldn't stop them. They flowed freely as I tried to hide the muffled sounds of my lungs pulling in the air.

"How long have you been here?" I closed my eyes, the tears burning the corners of my nose.

"I don't know. I lost track of the time. Maybe a few weeks? A month? What month is it?" The tears continued to build behind my eyelids, and I finally swallowed as hard as I could to stop the cry from coming out of me.

"It's October," I told her. I'm not sure what day though." I placed my hand back over my mouth, biting down on my lips to cry in silence. She erupted beyond the wall between us.

"October," she cried out. "God, what the fuck is happening? It was late August, I think. It's all getting blurry to me," she told me as she cried.

We sat in silence for a moment, knowing that we were both crying. As the thought of someone sitting in the dark, surrounded by the blasting music for over a month began to work its way through my mind, a loud shudder came from beyond the wall behind me. I stood up, feeling the walls begin to shake around me.

"Oh God," the girl said, her voice taking a serious tone. "Fuck, we have to get out of here. Now!" The wall to my left began to rattle from what sounded like her body pushing against it. "We have to leave here now before he comes back!"

I stepped back, her screams getting louder.

"Help me!"

I started to push against the wall, kicking the bottom of it as hard as I could.

"I'm trying!" I kicked the bottom corner of the wall between us as hard as I could, the baseboards on the bottom of it starting to give way, the rotting wood cracking. "I can't kick any harder!"

"Just keep kicking!" She screamed as she kicked from the other side. The sound from outside the room had stopped, but she kept pushing into the wall, the rotting bards turning into shards at my feet. "We can do it, just keep going!"

A small piece of the wood gave way at the bottom as my right foot connected with it, the toe of my boot going through it. I pulled back on the boot, stuck in the bottom of the wood, pinching my toes from the inside as I retracted it.

"There!" She screamed, her fingers coming from the small hole my boot created.

"I see it!" I knelt down and touched my hand to her fingers. "Keep kicking it from your side," I shouted at her. I'll pull from the bottom! I reached my hand through the tight crack and began to pull back toward myself, small pieces breaking off at a time. We were doing it, the wall was starting to break into small splinters. The more I pulled on the small cracks of broken wood, the more it gave way, giving enough room for both of my hands to go under the wall between us. After the girl gave another kick, the bottom panel of wood began to shake loose, the piece now flimsy enough to be pulled off the remainder of the wall.

"Pull it!" She screamed, placing her hands under the broken piece and pulling it toward her. The piece snapped off and she fell backward into the room she was in. I knelt down, placing my hands on the floor and leaning my head to the ground to look under the remaining wall.

"Are you okay?" A stupid question. No, she wasn't okay. Neither of us was. She sat back up and her hands grabbed mine. I still couldn't see her in the darkness, just the outline of her. My hands felt something warm and wet on the ground between us, and when I pulled my hands back toward me I realized they were covered in blood. Her blood. I gasped, rubbing my hands on my pants.

"I'm okay! We have to get the fuck out of here! Right now!" She was shouting, still pulling on the next piece of wood paneling when the music began to blare. "No! Please, God, no!" The beat rattled the wall that separated us, as she stood up.

I could only see her feet now, kicking against the other side of the wall as hard as she could, still screaming. I didn't know how to react. I didn't know if I should be screaming, or if I should shrink back into the darkness quietly. I couldn't choose which option was safer. I froze, watching her legs kick at the rotting wood beams, my teeth chattering again. She kicked the wall one last time before a light came on in the room she was in, the yellow glow seeping under the cracked boards.

Her feet stopped kicking, and I watched as they raised from the ground like she was being lifted into thin air. Her scream barely escaped her before it was stopped, her body slammed into the wall between us. Her feet dangled in the open piece of broken boards before me, the toes of her shoes barely able to touch the floor, slipping back and forth in the pool of blood that was now beginning to bleed into my room. I threw my body back into the wall behind me and clasped my hands over my mouth. Her body hit the floor with a thud, and the lights went off. Before I could stop myself, I was on my feet, kicking at the wall between us, screaming at the top of my lungs.

"Clinton, you coward! I will fucking kill you!" I couldn't stop myself. A rage took over me as I continued to scream, kneeling down and reaching my hands through the wall toward her body. I grabbed her arm and pulled her closer to the opening between the wall. Her skin was cold, the blood that covered her the only warm thing about her. I tapped at her, my voice echoing around the room as I screamed for Clinton to come back.

"Let me out of here you coward! You pussy!" I couldn't control myself, screaming any and everything that came into my head, words that would never have been used if not for this situation. I don't know if it was fear or anger that was fueling me, but I was getting out of here one way or another.

Chapter Twenty-Two
Girl in The Pines

The woods came into focus as she opened her eyes. It was barely light out, but the sound of birds filled the pines. She could feel the ground beneath her, the rocks pushing into parts of her back, her head to the side, her cheek against the Earth. The chirps and whistles engulfed her, and her eyes were barely able to stay open.

She didn't know where she was anymore, not that she ever really did. There was no telling how far she had come, or if she was any further than she had been. Everything was twisted within the woods. There was no sense of direction or time any longer. Her senses faded away, and now it all blurred together into this nightmare that surrounded her. The base of the tree trunks rose up around her like pillars, towering over her body. The ground was cold, and the sharp pieces of sticks and stones that poked into her only served as a reminder that she was still alive.

The thought of life itself felt more than unfortunate to her now.

She could feel the cool air burning her throat every time her body involuntarily took a breath, her exhales forming small clouds that lifted out of her, rising up into the trees. Images of home sifted in and out of her, her eyes feeling heavier with every thought that crossed her mind. She could stay here on the forest floor, let the Earth finally take her. It was only the idea of her home that kept her from letting the darker thoughts completely take over her.

The ground is safe. Giving up is safe, she thought.

The young girl's face from inside the cabin felt like it was burning itself into the back of her eyelids, the flashes of her hand reaching out for help knocked the cold air from her lungs. She really was beautiful, her face just as striking while covered in blood as it was in her missing fliers. She recognized her almost immediately.

Now, as she lay quiet in the middle of the woods, her face was all she could think about. She couldn't die here, not with the truth dying with her. She knew that. It was what she continued to tell herself in the moments she felt like giving up. Her body and her mind were no longer working together, her body was comfortable here on the cold ground, her mind a never-ending loop of reasons she had to live.

Chapter Twenty-Three

Eyvette

I kicked again, harder and harder with every swing of my leg. I knew she was dead, but I had to get to her. I noticed after a brief moment of fear between my screams, that the small door that entered her small room was left ajar. I couldn't make anything out in her room, but it seemed to be an exact match to mine, completely made of rotting wood panels, a small light cord hanging from the ceiling, and blood painted across the walls.

I kicked, my toes starting to hurt as my boot made contact with the bottom of the remaining wall. When the next panel began to shake, I kicked it again, my boot following it through as it dropped into her room. It wasn't a large gap, but big enough that I could squeeze myself through it if I lay flat.

I dropped to the floor, my hands scraping across the shards of wood that lined my side of the room. I could feel the blood soaking into my shirt and making contact with my skin as I tried to slip my arms through the opening, pulling myself through the wall. I reached back as my hair began to pull on the pieces of broken wood, and I ripped what felt like clumps out of myself to free my head from the crack between the rooms. My hands slipped across the rotting wood floor, warm and covered in what I knew to be blood. I still could only see the ground before me. I placed my hands against the wall surrounding my waist, and I pushed, squeezing my stomach in and trying to shift my hips just enough to allow myself through the opening. My pants caught on each piece of jagged wood, the shards scraping against my skin, opening small cuts along my waist. I pushed one last time, and the right side of my body slipped through the rest of the broken wood, taking the final panel off of the wall as I relaxed on the floor.

The blood had spread all around me, and no matter where my hands fell, they were met with warmth. I turned myself over and pulled my legs through the remaining wood, sliding my knees toward my chest. This room seemed identical to mine, but more light sifted in between the cracks that lined the blood-splattered walls. I could feel her arm pressed against my leg, her skin starting to feel cold.

I stood myself up and allowed the wood to scrape against my back as I slid myself up the wall for balance. I reached my hands all around me, feeling my way around the square room. I reached my hands as high as they could, the tips of my fingers finally wrapping themselves around the singular bulb that swung on an electrical cord. This light was different from the one in the room I had escaped. It hung much lower, and as my hands traced the shape of the bulb, I could feel a small switch on the side. I reached higher, my toes still hurting from kicking the wall. I grabbed the light with one hand and used the other to twist the small switch on the side.

The moment the switch turned, the warm yellow light inside the bulb started to glow. Flickering on and off, the light burned my eyes. It didn't matter, I continued to stare at the light, praying it wouldn't completely go out. I stood with the palms of my hands pressed into the wall behind me, and I took a few deep breaths. I wasn't ready to look down at her. I wasn't ready to know I was alone in this room with a dead girl. My lips began to quiver while I took the deepest inhale I could muster.

I looked down.

The floor was coated in a thick and moving layer of her blood. It pooled around her head. She lay face down on the wooden floor, her hands by her side. Thick golden brown hair lay in tangles all around her, twigs and leaves scattered throughout it. She was no bigger than I was, her body fit and covered in small cuts. The blood matted in her hairline, just above her right ear, the source of the pool beneath her on the floor. He had thrown her into the wall with enough force to shatter her. I knelt down, my hands shaking, tears free-flowing from my face. I reached for her arm and lifted her from under her shoulder. Her body rolled over, turning her cheek to rest on the rotting floor. I gasped, the wind almost completely knocked out of my lungs. She was beautiful, even in death, her face instantly recognizable.

Meredith Bates lay on the floor before me, eyes open, lifeless, and no longer missing.

CHAPTER TWENTY-FOUR
GIRL IN THE PINES

S he was running again, the trees parallel to her, her eyes barely able to see them until they were right in front of her. The forest was dark again, but the moonlight peeking through the cracks in the pines allowed just enough light to see a few feet in front of her. Everything was numb, the cold wrapping itself around her again. Every time her feet hit the Earth below, they were met with rocks, sticks, and rough ground.

The forest was alive tonight, the cicadas roaring around her like they had before. Owls would screech from out in the distance, farther than she could see. She could hear the sounds of animals moving through the woods, their footsteps creating small movements of leaves and pine needles. She could hear the tops of the trees moving in the breeze, and the faint sound of water rushing nearby. She stopped, breathing heavily, and closed her eyes to try and find where the sound was coming from.

A stream, maybe a river or a waterfall.

If she could find it in the dark, maybe she could follow it out of the woods. Her left ear could hear the water more clearly, and before there was time to change her mind, she took off in that direction. The denim shirt she somehow still had on was rigid, cold, and hard from the dried blood that now stained most of it. As she ran, she wondered if she would ever feel warm again. If she would ever feel safe.

She was smarter than this, at least she thought she was.

CHAPTER TWENTY-FIVE

EYVETTE

I could feel the blood on the floor around me starting to get colder as it soaked its way through the bottom of my pants. I felt it, but I wouldn't move. I couldn't. The pieces of broken wood in the wall behind me grabbed at my shirt as I tried to brace myself against it.

She was dead. Meredith Bates was dead. Her eyes held their gaze in my direction, still wide and frozen in fear. Her missing flier was striking, her hair pulled up behind the bandana, and her backpack strapped to her. She had entered the woods with a smile on her face, unaware that it would be the end of her. I thought of Charlie, and how much she must have cared for her to risk her own safety just for a chance to be with her. Meredith must have been worth it for her. I wondered what all she told Charlie about her relationship with Clinton.

Clinton Bates, the murderer who bashed me over the head and trapped me here just to watch him kill his own wife. He would never let me out of here alive, not now. The tears that fell down my face slipped down the sides of my nose and rose over my lips before falling off. Something in my chest felt tight, stopping me from inhaling deeply.

I closed my eyes and thought of Izzy, how awful it would be for her when she got the news. Knowing that the last things we said to each other weren't from a place of kindness. I wondered if she would hate me for the rest of her life, knowing that she warned me more than once that this had all been a stupid idea. She was right, she always was. Yet, I ignored her.

I had left her to come here, and for what? I couldn't do anything with the information I had. There was no way out that I could imagine. Clinton Bates was going to see to it that this story never got out. I was the one loose end he could tie up before slipping back into society as the sad husband whose wife was missing.

The light that still hung above me flickered on and off, creating a strobe effect that made Meredith's face look like it was moving toward me. I knew it wasn't, but every time I opened my eyes, hers were staring directly into mine. The tears were gone now, replaced by the tightness in my chest taking over my entire body. I was numb. But more than that, I was angry, furious. I wondered if Clinton had just awoken one day to decide that it was better to kill his wife than to let her divorce him and be free. To let her walk away with some shred of dignity after the abuse she had suffered at his hand. I had known that he couldn't be trusted.

From the moment I saw him on television, to the morning in the coffee shop, nothing he said sat right with me. It wasn't until the night of the storm that I truly started to question whether I had gotten him wrong. I hadn't, and I let him get close to me. I allowed him to twist my thoughts and get in my head. I shouldn't have gone back for the recorder. I should have pushed on and continued to run until I reached someone who could help me.

The story would have come out, and he would have been under more scrutiny than he was already. Whether people believed me or not, I would have told the facts that I knew were true, and the internet and all its glory would have done the rest. He would have never seen another peaceful day, I knew that.

The light above me flickered one last time, then went out. The image of Meredith's face still burned behind my eyes. The silence lasted a mere second before the music rattled the wall behind me. The bass violently shook the floorboards under me, its jagged edges cutting into my legs as I pushed against the ground.

I wouldn't scream, not out of fear this time. I wasn't afraid. If I was going to die then I'd die escaping this place. I would fight. I would try. I would claw my way out if I had to. We were able to break away at the bottom of the wall between our connected rooms, so there had to be a way to get me out. With the music so loud, I could kick and pull at the boards without him hearing me. I didn't know if Clinton was nearby, or watching my every move, but it was the only thought that drove me to keep fighting. If he came anywhere near me, I'd scratch, kick, bite, and punch my way into whatever outcome there was for me. I wouldn't lay here and die. I wouldn't give him the satisfaction. Not anymore.

I placed my hands on the wall near the door and began to kick again, pain shooting up my leg. Something was broken. But I kicked, over and over again, the bottom of the door rattling and then coming back to its starting position. I knelt down and peeled away at the wood chips that ran the length of the door frame. Bit by bit, small pieces began to chip away, creating a small hole just like the one before. I stood myself back up and took a deep breath, preparing my foot for the pain. I kicked with all the force I could muster, slamming my body into the door as I did. The pain radiated up my ankle and through my leg, but I continued to kick, breaking the small boards into little pieces that fell to the floor.

When I finally was able to get the toe of my boot through the small hole I had created, I dropped to the floor, my legs slipping in the thickening blood that coated the boards beneath me. I reached my hand through the door and pulled it toward me, my hand slipping back with nothing in it. I reached through again and pulled once more, bringing with me a piece of the wood panel. I clawed at the opening, my nails digging into each shard of wood, breaking it piece by piece. The music continued to shake the room while I worked away at the broken piece. I could feel the splinters of wood beneath my nails, tearing away at my fingertips. I knew the pain was there, but it wasn't registering to me.

All I could think about was getting out of this room. After that, I didn't know where I would go. How far I would have to run, or which direction to take off in. I had no clue where I was, or if I was in the woods at all anymore.

I pulled, and I pulled again until my entire hand and forearm were able to slip through the bottom of the broken board. I reached through until my elbow hit the broken wood, raising my hand up on the other side of the door and feeling around. The hole wasn't big enough for me to reach my entire arm through. I had to reach farther to see if there was any type of door handle. I pushed as hard as I could, the cracks pinching the skin on my arm, the burn of punctured skin radiating up the backside of my elbow. I pulled my arm back toward me, but it wouldn't budge.

I began to panic as I pulled on my arm, the skin still wedged between the cracks in the broken board. In the process of pulling, the pain in my feet and hands returned. The small rips and tears in my flesh burning. I turned to my side and placed my feet against the wall to push with all my remaining strength. The force sent a pop down my arm, but I felt the wood release. A shooting pain ran down my arm, tingling my fingers. Broken. I didn't know what, and I didn't know where, but I broke something in the process of freeing my arm from the door.

I crawled back into the corner of the small room. I could feel my strength starting to fade. I was tired, cold, and hungry. If I didn't get out now, there was no knowing that I would have the energy or another chance. I forced myself into a standing position and ran full force at the door in front of me.

CHAPTER TWENTY-SIX
GIRL IN THE PINES

All she could feel was the dried blood caked into her denim shirt, scratching her up and down as she ran. The previously soaked parts of her shirt were now rigid. Her body burned as if it were on fire. The rough pieces of her shirt sent shivers down her spine with every brush against her sensitive skin.

She shook her arms, freeing her shoulders from the confines of the shirt, and then, with one final swing, let it drift behind her as she ran.

Chapter Twenty-Seven

Eyvette

The door split down the centerboard, two connected panels falling with me through its threshold. I hit the floor, my shoulder landing just on top of a shattered board. The music muffled what I would assume had been a breaking sound, followed by a heavy thud. My adrenaline was pumping, enough that any and all pain I had experienced in the small room had drifted away from me. I lay on the floor, my eyes wide open, covered in shards and splinters of rotting wood. My breath was heavy, and my heart was racing. I could feel every inch of my body as if some electrical current of energy was passing through me. I rolled myself over and turned onto my knees, lifting myself to a standing position. The boards below me made me stumble until I found my way against the outside wall of the room I had just escaped.

I searched around the room, looking for any source of light I could find. I followed the wall with my hand as I stepped around the broken boards, careful not to trip over them again.

The beat of the music continued, shaking the wall I balanced myself against. I had only taken a few steps when my right foot hit something on the floor, sending my body crashing into the hardwood. I barely had time for my hands to meet the ground before I realized I had fallen. My legs were suspended behind me, hanging over whatever it was I had tripped over. The feel of it against my legs sent a shiver down my spine. I knew what it was without seeing it.

A body.

A large body, thick and solid.

I quickly pulled my legs toward me, staring at the shadowed outline on the floor. *Who was it? Were they dead?* I couldn't gather my thoughts as they raced away inside of me. I was out of the room, but I still wasn't alone.

Against my better judgment, I crawled toward the body and reached my hand out toward it. My fingers were met with a cold rubber touch, and I knew at that moment that whoever this was, they were dead. I pulled my hand back reactively and heard the sound of something rolling across the floor. I reached in its direction, wrapping my hands around its handle. A flashlight. I held it up to my face and felt around the cylindrical handle, searching for the switch. My thumb grazed over it, and with a click, the beam of light shot from it. The lens was cracked, sending streaks of light in different directions.

It was Clinton Bates' flashlight, dried mud and all.

I held it in my hand for a moment, just staring at it, sending a painful reminder to the crack that ran the length of my face. I turned the beams of light toward the floor, following the glow with my eyes as it moved up the length of the body.

I screamed, barreling backward away from him. The music was so loud around me that it felt like I was trapped in a silent film. My mouth hung wide open, my scream erased by the blaring sounds. Tears streamed down my cheeks and collected on my chin while my hands shook under the weight of the flashlight.

It was Clinton Bates.

His eyes stared blankly into the abyss.

Throat sliced from ear to ear.

Blood, thick and oozing down his neck like some macabre drip cake.

I dropped to the floor and his flashlight landed beside me. I hurriedly reached for it again and held it up, the dim light landing on his prone body.

He was dead.

There was no blood surrounding him on the floor, and as I looked him over, I noticed how pale and blue his lips and face were. There was no way he had been killed here, not with his throat cut open like that. It looked as if he had been dead for days. Days, I thought. If he was dead, then who had killed Meredith? Who had put me into that room?

My thoughts flew around as I stared into his opened eyes. I cried, my chest shaking from the uneven amounts of air I was able to take in. I stood up, turned the flashlight out into the room, and looked all around the room. The door I had escaped from was one of three against the wall, two of them open, one of them still closed. I didn't see any other way to exit the room. I made my way around Clinton's body, still watching his face as I moved.

The door had a small hook for a handle, and as I placed my hand on it, I realized that it didn't move. I pulled it toward me, the door not budging. I put the flashlight into my mouth, holding it between my teeth, the light still shining toward the door. I used both of my hands, pulling the hook with all the strength I had left. The door was solid, not moving in the slightest as I pulled it. Out of frustration alone, I kicked the bottom of the door, hopeful that I could break through it like I had twice before.

Over the music, I heard the faint sound of a scream. I stopped kicking, dropping to the floor, and turning off the flashlight. I braced myself, placing my ear up against the door. I could hear her crying. I knocked on the base of the door, hoping she could hear me over the music.

"Hello? Is someone there?"

Her cries stopped, as the faint sound of scuffling came from the floor on the other side of the door. I could barely hear her, but she was there.

"Hello? Please help me! Please, God, help me," she said through the door.

"I'm trying! I'm going to try and kick the door again! When you see any light coming through, start pulling on the wood!"

"No, please! He will hear us! Please!" She was desperate, her voice shaking.

"It's just me here," I told her. "I can get you out of here, just please help me!" I didn't wait for her to respond. I stood up and began to kick the base of the door as hard as I could. I could feel the board starting to give as my foot slammed into it for the third and fourth time. The moment the piece of board snapped at the kick of my toe, I dropped to the floor, sticking my fingers through the crack and pulling. Her hands were coming through the opening to help pull toward her. She was crying again, and I could barely hear her over the music and snapping of rotting wood.

"Keep pulling," I yelled to her. "Don't stop!"

Her hands were covered in what looked like dried blood. They would come through the crack in the board, feel around for a good grip, and then pull back toward her, taking with them small pieces of splintering wood. With both of us pulling it apart, it began to shred, opening the hole wider.

I stood back up and yelled at her to watch her hands, stepping back and taking a running start to kick the board one last time. My foot made contact and fell through the opposite side of the door with the cracked wood. I lost my balance and fell to the ground, quickly gathering myself back to my hands and knees to bring my face down.

"Yvee," the girl said before her face came into focus in the beam of the flashlight that now lay on the floor beside me.

I picked it up and flashed it in the direction of the hole in the door. Her hair was covered in dried blood, matted, and stuck to her face.

"Charlie?" I leaned closer to the ground. "Holy fuck, is that you, Charlie?" I moved closer to the hole, recognizing the shape of her face immediately. "Oh my God, Charlie!"

"Yvee, how are you here? How did you find me?" We were practically screaming at one another through the broken beam in the door, trying to be louder than the music that still rattled the walls.

"Charlie, we have to get you out of there. We have to go!" I was starting to pull on the rotting board again as she reached her hand out to touch mine.

"Yvee, you have to go. You have to leave right now!" Tears were streaming down her face. I stopped ripping the board for a moment to make eye contact with her.

"I am not going to leave you here, Charlie. We have to get you out of there now!" The moment I said it, I could finally hear how loud I was screaming. The music had come to a complete stop, and silence fell around us both. I sat up and shot the beam of the flashlight around the room, waiting for whoever was keeping us here to come out for me.

"It's on a timer," she said, her voice cracking. "It goes off every two hours, I think." She sounded exhausted, her breath heavy, her words shaky. "I think," she repeated aloud to herself.

"Charlie, I'm going to get you out of there, I promise." I reached up toward the next beam and began to pull, my feet pressed against the outline of the doorframe. I pulled as hard as I could.

"You can't," she started crying. "You can't save me." Her hands kept pulling at mine, trying to stop me from my attempt to pull the next board off of the door.

"Stop it, Charlie! I'm getting you out of there!" She continued to cry, sitting back in the room where I could no longer see her. "Charlie!" I couldn't see her, the flashlight beam was not strong enough to shine to the farthest part of her room. I could hear the sound of chains being pulled across the floor from beyond the door. My hands stopped pulling the moment I could see her legs. Thick and rusted cuffs encased her ankles, both rubbed raw by the peeling metal on the chain. The flashlight glow shimmered off another chain, this one silver with no rust, that hung between both ankles, connecting the two cuffs. Another chain ran from her right ankle, and I followed it as far as I could until the darkness stopped my vision.

"You can't," she told me. "I'm not going anywhere."

Her cries broke me, but I tried to remain as calm as I could, pulling at the board again.

"Yes, I can!"

"Yvee! You have to go! You have to get yourself out of here, he will come back!"

I continued to pull, talking between the choppy breaths I could take.

"Eyvette, he will kill you! Do you understand me!" She was yelling, her cries sounding angrier as I pulled.

"Who? Who will kill me Charlie, who's doing this?

"I don't know," she said, wiping tears away from her dirty face, her hands the deepest of red from the dried blood. "I thought I did, but it's not him!" She lifted her hands and pointed them in the direction of the dead body behind me. "He killed him the moment he brought him here. I didn't know it was you, I couldn't hear anything over the music," she cried to me. "I watched through the crack as he took him outside," she began to tell me as I pulled on the board again. "The moment he came back, he was dragging him in here, I knew he was dead. I thought it was him the whole time, Yvee. I swear I did." Her voice stopped as a sob worked its way up from deep inside of her. "I thought I'd done this." She broke, her body bending forward as she cried into her red hands. "Is she dead?" She heaved, her body rocking back and forth as the tears created skin-colored lines down her face. "She is, isn't she?"

"No," I lied to her. I couldn't have her giving up more than she already was. "She must have gotten out, it's just us in here."

She swallowed hard and tried to stop herself from crying.

"Are you sure?"

I couldn't look directly at her. I wouldn't be able to lie to her again.

"It's just us, Charlie. We have to get out of here!" I could feel the board starting to wiggle ever so slightly. "Help me!" She moved toward me and grabbed the board from inside the room.

"Yvee, how are we going to get these chains off of me?"

I didn't answer her. I just continued to pull the piece of wood until it finally ripped away from the door. I bent over and pulled her toward me, her arms feeling so weak in my hands.

"He's gonna come back, Yvee, he's not going to let us leave!"

"Who?" I reached up and grabbed her face, staring into her eyes. "Who is coming back? Who is he?"

"I don't know! I can never see his face, it's always cov-ered with a black mask. He doesn't say anything at all," she told me.

I crawled my way around her into the small room she was in, pulling the flashlight in behind me. It was exactly the same as the room I had been kept in, her walls covered in dried blood. The chains that connected to the cuffs on her ankles ran the length of the floor and then dropped into a hole that had been drilled into the floor. I reached for her ankle chains, pulling at them. Charlie winced in pain, causing me to pull my hands away from her immediately. Her ankles were bruised, covered in dried blood, and swollen from the metal cuffs starting to cut their way into her skin. I felt myself trying to stop a painful look from showing across my face.

"I'm sorry, Charlie, I know it hurts, but I have to get you out of here." She reached out and pulled me into her. It felt as if I could feel every bone in her body. Her shoulders dug into my arms as I held her. "I'm so sorry."

"We're going to die here," she said, her head folding into my shoulders. She cried again, and I began to push her off of me. I couldn't let her go there.

"No! Charlie, we are going to get out of here, do you hear me? My Black ass isn't about to die in this room. Not here, not like this, and not with your hair doing whatever this is," I reached up and touched her hair, which felt as dry as straw. I laughed with her. It was all I could do. My attempt at a joke was the only thing keeping me from breaking into tears. She let out a small laugh, just barely audible. "Listen, we just have to be smart here."

She nodded at me, understanding that I wasn't going to accept any other answer from her.

I continued to pull at the cuffs on her, realizing that there was no way of removing them from her with just my hands. They were solid, and even though they were covered in rust, they were too strong for someone to just pull them apart.

"I have to find something to get these off of you," I told her, aiming the flashlight out of the broken doorway.

"No! Please don't leave me, Yvee! Please, please just stay here."

I turned back toward her, her face with a look of pure terror.

"Please," she said again.

"Charlie, I will be right back, do you hear me? I will be right back. I have to find something to break these chains." I reached for her face, placing my hand on her cheek. "I promise."

I slipped my way through the bottom of the doorway, and stood up, the flashlight beam tracing the walls of the room. I walked slowly, following the wall to my left, carefully shining the light toward the ground as I stepped. I made my way around a small table with a broken leg, as the flashlight lit a large bowl with what looked like rotting food inside of it. I moved around it, checking underneath it as I did. I could see a set of shelves just ahead of me, and as I reached my hands toward them, the music began to rattle the shack again.

I dropped to the floor, clicking the flashlight off, pulling my knees toward me, and pressing myself into the wall below the shelves. The soft glow of the flashlight had just gone off when a crack on the other side of the room appeared. A door opened slowly as a large man stepped into its frame. From where I was under the shelves, I watched him duck his head as he stepped through the doorway into the room, his head higher than the highest beam above it. I could feel myself holding my breath, one hand holding the flashlight, the other over my mouth.

The light from beyond the open door sent rays of sunlight across the floor in front of him, my legs just beyond its reach. I prayed he wouldn't turn on any type of light. The door shut behind him as he stepped his way through the threshold. As it closed, I got to my knees and began to crawl my way toward it.

Charlie was still in the small room, chained to the floor.

I told myself that if I could get out of this room, just beyond that door, I could get help. As I crawled, my mind raced with how I could run in any direction until I found someone, counting my steps and watching the trees I passed. I would remember each and every step, so I could lead someone back to this place.

I would keep my promise to her.

I wouldn't just leave her here.

My thoughts came to a stop the moment lights began to beam throughout the room. The music had stopped, the floor and walls around me now visible. I reached out toward the door frame, close enough for my fingers to touch its rotting wood. I felt my body get shoved to the side just as my hand made contact with it.

A burning pain radiated its way across my side, just above my hip. Just as my body hit the ground, I could feel the knife going into my side once more. I rolled to my back as the air was knocked out of me. He stood over me, chains dangling from his hands. His fists were clenched around them, and as he raised them over his head, I could feel my hips rising from the ground. The higher he lifted, the more I moved. I tried to scream, but everything was going black around me.

I turned my head toward the broken door on the other side of the room, as Charlie reached her hands out from under it, her eyes wide, a scream erupting from her that I couldn't make out over the music.

I closed my eyes.

CHAPTER TWENTY-EIGHT

GIRL IN THE PINES

I was still running, this time for her.

I left her.

I knew there was nothing I could do, but I hated myself for leaving her.

She knew it, too. She knew there was nothing I could do. She begged me to leave her there, yelling at me to go over and over again. I would have stayed with her. I would have died right there in that dark room.

My hands were no match against the chains that bound her. Now, there was nothing left for me to give the world. Nothing but the truth of what I had seen. I ran, even though my body told me to stop. To fall to the ground and die.

The sounds of the woods echoed all around, and from somewhere behind me, I heard someone yell. A low, guttural yell that set the hair on my neck to a standing position. I kept running, the yell growing into a scream.

The Earth below me was starting to soften, and my feet sank further into the wet soil. I wouldn't stop, not again. My lungs burned, unable to provide me a deep enough breath to calm myself. I cried, my eyes burning as the trees passed me by one by one. I promised myself that if

I made it out of the woods, I'd never step foot into them ever again. I would trust my gut feelings, and I'd listen to them.

The woods began to separate and glow as I pushed myself through the soft ground, the darkness being taken over by light cutting through the trees. A field, I thought. There's nowhere else to go, but I knew there would be nowhere to hide out in a field. I'd be an open target for whoever was chasing me.

I screamed, my body begging me to stop running.

I wouldn't.

It didn't matter. Whoever was chasing me knew exactly where I was, they knew the Pines, and they knew that I couldn't run forever.

I ran through the last two large pines, my feet lifting off of the ground as it began to drop down on a slope. I was airborne, my legs still kicking as I flew through the air. The ground rose up to meet me, my legs slamming into the ground. The wind was knocked out of me. I got myself to my knees and crawled forward.

There was a large drainage ditch just beyond me, and past that, what looked like an opening to another trail. As hard as I tried, the air my body wouldn't let me breathe in, my chest and sides cramping. I pressed my hands into the ground and threw myself forward, my feet catching the ground and raising me up into a running position. My hands ripped away at the vines and brush that surrounded the ditch. I clawed through them, pushing my body forward as they snapped against me. My body toppled forward again, and I raised my head from the other side of the ditch. My eyes wandered from left to right, watching the opening stretch across the pines.

Not a trail, but a road. Run down, and poorly paved, but there.

I looked to the right, the road curving around the trees. It was going downhill, and that was all it took for my body to push me to my feet again. I was running down the paved road, my feet no longer sticking to the ground. Gravity pulled me down faster than I would have been able to run, and there were moments when I thought my body would outrun my feet. I didn't care anymore. If the pavement met my face, I would take it like I had taken every other hit. If I was going to cry, I was going to cry while I ran.

Pain, cold, and this goddamn forest wasn't going to stop me.

The road wound around the pines, curve after curve. The cracks in the pavement caught my feet as I ran, tripping me for a few steps before I would inevitably regain my composure. It was the first time in days that I felt any hope at all. The morning sun was barely eclipsing the horizon, the forest still dark all around me. I ran, following the turns around the road as the hill kept me moving forward.

I thought of all the women this forest had consumed in its secrets. How they would enter the forest unaware of their fates. How they would hike into the beautiful hills and find comfort in the Pines, completely unaware that they were being watched; and hunted.

The trees would conceal anyone that was lurking around them, following their movements from behind the brush, using the sound of the woods to mask their noises. I thought of them both, how they would die in that cabin.

I saw her face flash through my mind, her hands reaching out as I turned to run.

My body shook at the thought. Every muscle I had vibrated as I ran, each trying its hardest to maintain motion.

I thought of her, her body tired and weak, wrapped in chains.

I could run for the rest of my life and would never outrun the guilt of leaving her behind. He would kill her if he hadn't already. Leaving her meant letting her die. I shook my head as I ran, sending the thoughts out of my mind.

The road began to level out, the incline slowly dissipating. My body felt heavy, but I kept my eyes on the horizon line. The sun was coming up, sending purple and orange hues throughout the morning sky.

Another morning.

Another night alive in the Pines.

I could feel the tears running down the sides of my face. Before I could stop myself, I was standing completely still in the middle of the road. Just ahead of me, barely visible, a light grew larger and larger. As it approached me, I could hear the rumbling of its engine. I stood motionless, watching as it made its way in my direction, its multicolored lights starting to spin in circles atop its roof.

A police car.

My body heaved, my heart almost exploding in my chest as I watched it come to a stop.

The door opened, and a tall bearded man stepped out in complete shock. For a moment, he could only stare at me, his words suffocated by the sight of me.

I looked in all directions around me, wondering if any of this was real. Was I just imagining the safety of someone finding me and rescuing me from the Pines?

My eyes watched the edge of the woods, waiting for whoever was doing this to grab me.

Chapter Twenty-Nine
Eyvette

S he hung from the chains, side still burning from the blows of the knife.

Charlene, she was alive, at least she had been. She had seen her, touched her, and spoken to her before the lights went out again.

The metal chains holding her in place dangled around her, scraping the floor. Her head pounded, blood flowing in the direction of the floor. It trickled down her sides and pooled beneath her hair on the floor. She didn't know how long she had been hanging upside down. The music raged on, rattling all around her through the thick chain that weaved itself in and out of her limbs. She tried to move her head up, lifting it as far as she could. The large chains ran in all directions around her, and as she followed them with her tired eyes, she saw them.

Hooks.

She could feel the pressure and burning in her sides and had assumed it was from the blow of a knife. That he had stabbed her. These weren't wounds from a knife.

No, she was suspended by large hooks that entered her body on both sides of her hips. She winced from the pain, barely able to keep her eyes open. She was dizzy, and her head still rushed from the blood that gravity continued to pull downward. She could feel her heart trying to speed up in fear, but it didn't. It couldn't.

She told her to run. She begged her to. She was all that mattered anymore. She was safe. She had to be. She was right, this was a stupid mistake.

A mistake that had turned into a nightmare.

She would die here in the Pines, just like the other girls.

Charlene screamed from behind the closed door, her cries muted only by the beat of the music. It was almost comforting now and she found herself closing her eyes. She could feel the music rattling its way through the chains that wrapped her. Her focus was on home, on the only person she loved in the world.

She took a deep breath, her mind alight with all the what-ifs.

None of them mattered anymore.

The words to the music playing were still unintelligible, but they brought tears that flowed from her eyes, up her forehead before dripping to the floor, falling into blood. She opened her eyes and screamed one last time. She closed her eyes again, wondering if anyone would ever know the very last song she heard before she died.

Chapter Thirty

Girl in the Pines

"I'm Sheriff Burke. What's your name sweetheart?" His voice was raspy, my eyes were still focused on the edge of the woods.

Someone had always been behind me.

Something had been there.

I could hear them.

I could feel them around me as I ran.

I stood motionless, my body finally giving out. I couldn't move. He stepped toward me, and I stepped back for just a moment, letting my eyes travel up and down him. He was handsome if you were into scruffy men who wore clothing a little too tight to show off their physique. I took a deep breath and felt my body giving out. I wasn't alone, not anymore. I felt his arms wrap around me as my body slumped into him, all of my weight finally falling forward.

"Whoa, it's going to be okay. Can you tell me your name?"

I closed my eyes, my body feeling everything all at once.

"My name..." I started, my throat ached from screaming. "My name is..." My mind had completely melted, everything rushing into me all at once. He held me, pressed against him, as I finally looked up toward him, attempting to use my arms to stand again. My muscles had all finally given out, and my body felt like it was made of lead.

"It's okay, you're safe," he told me. "How long have you been out here? You must be freezing." He lifted me from the ground and walked me toward the side of the car. The lights still rotated as he opened the door and slid me into the passenger seat.

"The lights," I said. "He'll see the lights."

He shut the door and walked around the car, opening his door and sitting down.

"Who? Who will see the lights? Was someone with you?" He didn't understand. No one was with me, but I wasn't alone. I had never been alone since stepping foot into the pines.

"We have to go," I cried. "Please."

"Okay, okay, we're going. I've got you," he said as the car began to roll forward.

The car rumbled down the unevenly paved road, heading through the narrowing pines that towered over it. I was safe, my body feeling the warmth as it lifted its way from the floor of the car. I leaned my head against the window, my shallow breaths sending small outlines of fog across the glass.

The music played low in the background and I could feel my body filling with nausea. I blinked, watching the trees as they passed by in perfect lines. I wondered again if this was all just a nightmare that I would wake up from eventually.

"My name is Izzy," I told him. "Izzy Chambers."

My face could feel the coldness of the woods bleeding through the glass of the window as I pressed my face back into it. I closed my eyes and let the tears fall down my cheeks.

I knew they were dead.

That she was dead.

Even if I had been able to find my way back, there wouldn't have been enough time for them. The images of her flashed in my head again, this time unable to be shaken away.

Blood covered the floor around her as she screamed for me to go.

I grabbed her face, kissed her, and told her I loved her.

I had run for days to escape the woods, to escape him. I could hear her telling me to run over and over again as the trees began to move past us faster and faster. I had left her to die, just like Charlene Ellis. I had gotten away just as she begged me to. I had listened to her and found my way out of the woods. I took a deep breath, letting the nausea wash over me.

A steady beat began to make its way up the doorframe of the car, vibrating against my face. The car continued to follow the curves of the road, barreling through the Pines. I turned to face him, disoriented from the speed of the car. I didn't know if we were going away from, or deeper into the Pines.

The hair on my neck stood at attention as the music began to come into focus, my body tensing with every beat.

1-2-3-4, 1-2-3-4, boom boom boom.